BARE B
Flash Fiction

Compiled by Daizi Rae

volume three

Contributing authors in order of appearance:

Daizi Rae
Sandy Biddles
Carolyn Ward-Daniels
George Thomson
April Berry
Gerry O'Keeffe
JA Fabre
Jayne Love
Finbar Ansbe
Ceejhay Walker
Dean Wrigley
William Samson

INTRODUCTION

Welcome to the third volume of the Bare Books podcast's flash fiction anthology! we're about to take a joyride through the minds of some seriously talented listeners-turned-authors. I'm one of the podcast's co-hosts, along with April Berry, and let me tell you, we are absolutely over the moon about the support we got from you during season 6.

These stories are like the love children of our writing prompts and our listeners' imaginations - born to shine and dazzle. We're talking drama, mysteries, adventure, and heartwarming tales that'll give you all the warm fuzzies.

These bite-sized bursts of brilliance are your perfect sidekicks for a quick getaway during your daily grind, or a little breather on a crazy day.

Huge shout-out to all the amazing authors who filled these pages with their awesomeness, and to every book lover out there supporting our shenanigans by grabbing this anthology. Your enthusiasm compels us to continue exploring the endless depths of flash fiction storytelling.

So, grab a comfy spot, kick back, and let us entertain you. The magic of words is about to sweep you off your feet as we dive headfirst into endless possibilities. Enjoy the ride, my friend!

Daizi Rae

CONTENTS

CHAPTER ONE

The stories in this first chapter were inspired by a set of photographs taken by Daizi Rae on a walk along the beach in Withernsea in the UK. There were flowers strewn along the beach, lying across the sand and the stones. One of the stones looked like it had formed around a gold ring over the years. It's fascinating how any one image can spark so many different ideas and stories. I hope you enjoy reading them as much we enjoyed writing them...

VIOLET
Daizi Rae

Violet Wilson said goodbye to her lifelong friend, Mary Rutherford, at the front gate of their adjoining terrace houses on Church Street after their usual Saturday outing to the Knit and Natter group with the rest of the WI.

"It really was a fun one today, Mary. Maud was a riot, wasn't she? I thought she was gonna fall off that chair; she was laughing so hard," said Violet.

Mary grinned back at her. "Yeah, and Jenny scowled so hard at her behaviour, I'm amazed she didn't pop a vein. Who knew knitting could be such fun? Anyway, good night Violet, see you tomorrow."

"Yeah, Night Mary, sleep well, see you in the morning for church," replied Violet.

Violet let herself into her house, hung up her coat, and dropped her knitting bag on the hall table before pottering through to the kitchen and popping the kettle on the stove top for a bedtime cuppa with a kick of the good stuff. She took two steaming mugs upstairs and placed one on either side of the bed before going over to the bookcase, and pushing it along its sliders, revealing a hidden door. She tapped on the door and said, "I've made us a cuppa, love." The door opened and Mary stepped through, already in her nightgown from the bedroom next door.

"Ooh, you're a keeper," Mary said, dropping a kiss on Violet's lips. "It'll be the perfect temperature by the time you're ready for bed and snuggled under that eiderdown with me. Get a wriggle on, and I'll get the bed nicely warmed up for you."

Just as they were drifting off to sleep, Violet, snuggled up in Mary's arms as usual, said, "have a think about what you'd like to do next weekend. It's our Ruby anniversary; we should celebrate."

"I will, darling. Night-night, sweet dreams."

On their anniversary, Mary presented Violet with a watercolour painted by their very good friend and confidante, Thomas Middleton, of the Whitby Harbour. Tom was their neighbour on the other side of Violet's house and the only person in the whole world who knew their secret. In fact, he had known even before they had told him. "Oh ladies, you don't have to tell me," he'd said with a grin at the time, "the walls are paper-thin."

The ladies spent their special day at Whitby Harbour, then visited the Abbey and joked about buying a dog and calling him Stoker, in honour of Bram Stoker, who had written a book in their area. The dog had been an ongoing joke over the years, which was really only half a joke as Mary would have loved one, but their lifestyle didn't really lend itself to owning a dog. They had never spent a night apart in 40 years, and that night was no different. They made love until the early hours and drifted off to sleep wrapped up in each other as always.

***

As Jack sauntered along Church Street with Tilly, his beloved border collie, on their morning walk, he spotted Violet on her doorstep. He dropped her a wink as he said, "Morning, Violet love, how are you today?"

Violet smiled. "Morning, Jack, another blustery one, I see."

"Aye, lass, but at least the sun is shining today, and it's always that bit nicer when I see your smile of a morning."

Just then, Mary appeared on her doorstep next door. "Oh, looks like I timed it just right for a neighbourhood natter this morning. Morning, Jack; morning, Violet."

"Good morning, another beautiful face to brighten up my day," flirted Jack.

"Get away with you, Jack," giggled Mary as she stepped out of her gate to pop down to the grocers. "I bet you say that to all us old girls, eh, Violet?"

Mary stepped onto the road, still smiling. She didn't see the new Model T Ford car, and the driver, distracted and showing off his new car to his passenger, didn't see her until it was too late. Jack rushed to Mary's side and did his best to help, and Violet cried Mary's name over and over as she dropped to her knees beside her love, willing her to open her eyes. The noise on Church Street went from screeching metal, shouts for help, and the slamming doors of the neighbours running to help, to utter silence as everyone stood shocked. The silence was broken only by Violet's quiet sobs as they waited for an ambulance to arrive.

***

On what would have been Violet and Mary's forty-first anniversary, Violet walked along the beach towards Whitby Harbour with a bouquet of ruby red roses, dropping them one by one along the sand as she walked. On her coat, she wore a gold ring set inside a Whitby jet brooch in honour of Mary.

She couldn't bring herself to walk around the harbour today, so she turned around and called, "Come on, Stoker, let's go home. Good boy."

FLIGHT
Sandy Biddles

Foaming white waves rolled back and forth as Agnes Bone stood on the shore, lost in her dreams. Her shawl hung loosely, her bare legs and feet whipped by surges of sharp sand. Agnes yearned to be a bird, soaring away from the uncertainty of her fate.

Unaware of the storm brewing, she paid little attention to the darkening sky or the sense of urgency carried by the wind. The bay lay empty, devoid of any vessels on the horizon, and surprisingly, there were no cacophonies of sea birds - only the gentle lapping of waves reached her ears.

Suddenly, Agnes's reverie was shattered by a lilting voice calling her name. A diminutive, plump woman emerged, strolling among the dunes. Her wiry yellow hair resembled the wild gorse and was wrapped in a tawny cloak.

"What are you doing out here, dear? Your gown and flowers are laid out on your bed. We must hurry to the Kirk before the storm arrives," the woman said.

Agnes hesitated, abruptly snapped back to the present and feeling a chill down her spine. Eliza had been her surrogate mother for seventeen years, since her parents drowned and she was washed ashore as a six-month-old baby. Now, her life was about to take another turn. In this small community, a woman was expected to marry; her entire existence depended on it. Reluctantly, Agnes trudged back to the croft, her heart pounding. She couldn't help but think of the tiny, vulnerable heart of a bird, how it could sing and soar until it burst.

The croft was adorned with wreaths and garlands crafted from flowers and trees gathered from the garden and the nearby coppice. Agnes pondered that the Kirk would likely be similarly bedecked, and soon the community would gather, undeterred by the impending rain. A wedding was a welcomed diversion from the toil and labor of a crofter's life, an opportunity for feasting and dancing.

Gazing into the small mirror to adjust the flower garland lovingly made by Eliza, Agnes beheld a plain, serious face framed by long, straight, chestnut hair.

"I shall be a farmer's wife," she sternly reminded herself, suppressing the tears of self-pity welling up in her heart.

On the opposite side of the bay, Tam, a twenty-five-year-old in search of a wife, sat observing the storm as it loomed over the sea, bearing down on the island. Standing at six feet two, with a weathered brown complexion from a life spent outdoors, Tam had shouldered the responsibilities of the family farm after his father's passing.

However, marriage, especially one arranged for convenience, had never crossed Agnes's mind. When she wasn't assisting Eliza at the croft, she roamed the woods or wandered along the seashore, foraging, dreaming, and singing—a soul attuned to nature.

Huddled within their crofts, the islanders listened as the rain intensified, relentlessly pounding on the roofs and windows. Thunder and lightning clashed in a furious battle. Farmers hurried to seek shelter for their animals, while birds sought refuge wherever they could.

Eliza neither saw nor heard Agnes leave. Later, she would swear on the Holy Mary that she had bolted the front and back doors, with Eliza in the parlour and old man Partridge in the kitchen.

Agnes Bone was never found, and no boats had left their moorings. When the storm subsided on the following day, the island's men scoured the beach and woods. Near the dunes, Tam, still clad in his wedding suit, stumbled upon the wedding band, its brilliance dazzling as it slipped between the rocks.

Rising to his feet and continuing along the path to the woods, Tam failed to notice the wreath of red roses and peonies carried away by the tide, or the young sandpiper soaring from the rocks, singing of its newfound freedom.

THE BEACH BOUQUET
Carolyn Ward-Daniels

Petra Bowler was nine, and her sister Amy was seven. Petra had a colourful imagination, and Amy was only too happy to dive into her sister's fantasy world. They were now off for a seaside holiday, and Petra told Amy it was full of excitement.

In their caravan bedroom, they shared bunk beds and shared the thrills of the day: beach talk, funfair, and arcades. They weren't too far from the beach and would lie and listen to catch the sounds of the sea. When the tide was in, they could hear the pounding of the waves. The little voice in the bottom bunk said, "I'm scared. The waves were really big today."

Petra leaned over the top bunk. "What are you scared of?"

"What if the sea doesn't stop and it keeps coming? It will get us."

"It will stop, silly. It stops and goes back."

"What if it doesn't?"

"It will."

Amy listened to the pounding, thinking about what she had overheard in the arcade that day. "I heard two old men talking about the sea coming in. They talked about 'The big flood,' and one man put his hand over his head, saying, 'I was seven years old then, and it was this deep over my head. We all had to live upstairs until the sea went.'"

"How old did he look?"

"Old, like Granddad Bowler."

"So it was a long time ago."

"Yes, but I'm seven. What if the sea comes in again? There isn't an upstairs in the caravan."

Petra thought about this and tried to figure out how safe they would be, but Amy started snivelling, so she slid down from the top bunk and got into bed with her sister. It was much narrower than their beds at home, so they were sardined together. Amy thought Petra was clinging close to her because there was a real danger and snivelled some more.

"Don't cry."

"Are you scared as well?"

"No, the sea stops and goes back."

"How does it know to stop?"

Petra didn't know and thought hard for an answer. "You know the Earth?"

"Yes."

"Well, you know the Earth spins around?"

"Yes."

"Well, as it spins and tips to one side, the water of the sea runs that way."

"Where does it run to?"

"Probably Australia. So, like when our tide comes in, it goes out in Australia, and when it goes out here, it goes in over there, on the other side of the world."

"What if it tips the wrong way?"

"It never does. Anyway, the caravan will float; we'll have our own boat. It'll be brilliant."

Friday was the last day to go to the beach. A soil-faced cliff gave way to sand dunes, a promenade, and beach access. It was all sand pies, spades, and sandwiches. At half-past three, the girls were told they would be packing up soon.

Amy said she wanted to find some shells. Petra pointed to the bottom of the cliff. "There are some over there."

They took their buckets and footed about in the flotsam the night tide had left, and Petra nodded to the cliff, saying, "See, this is where the sea stops, Amy."

Amy looked at the sand littered with seaweed, and amongst the pebbles was a pitiful splat of flowers. "Look here," she said. Petra joined her. "Looks like that would have been a bouquet."

They stared at the sad-looking flowers, and Amy said, "Do you think someone threw them off the cliff?"

"Why would somebody do that?"

"Like if somebody had died."

Petra's eyes widened. "Ooooh," she added drama to her voice, "what if somebody fell off the cliff and died... or... or was pushed!"

"You mean somebody killed someone?"

"Could've."

They both stared up to the ridge and back at the distorted flowers. Petra's mind was on fire; her imagination needed little prompting. "Somebody murdered someone by pushing them off the cliff, then felt sorry and came back with flowers."

"Do you think it was a woman?"

"Definitely. I think women are easier to push off a cliff."

"Do you think she got washed out to sea?"

"Yes, she's probably in Australia by now."

They heard their mother call them. Petra scored a cross in the sand with her heel, pitched her hands in prayer, and said, "God bless." Amy said, "Amen."

They raced back to where their parents were packing up. The girls declared their need to go to the toilet.

"Off you go, stay together. We'll wait outside on the prom for you."

The girls talked through the thin partition walls of the cubicles, and their conversation floated under and over the gaps. "Do you think it was her husband that pushed her off the cliff?"

"Could've been. I mean, he brought flowers after the sea took her body away."

A woman at the washbasin dashed outside to tell her husband, who told the man next to him, who stood next to the girls' parents. Their mother went into the toilets as the girls washed their hands. "Come on, there's been an incident."

"What's an incident?"

"A woman's been swept out to sea. They think she's been murdered."

The girls looked at each other wide-eyed as their mother left. "We were right, Amy."

Outside, people were starting to group together on the promenade, arms pointing, heads shaking. The husband of the woman who had overheard the girls went over to the coastguard's office to make inquiries. The coastguard immediately phoned the police. The woman saw the girls coming out of the toilets and asked them, "You knew about the woman being murdered?"

Amy said, "Yes, our mom told us."

The crowd grew, and they decided to go back to the caravan. They walked through the sand dunes and heard sirens approaching and saw blue flashing lights.

Before they went to bed that night, Amy put the sink and basin plugs firmly in the holes and closed the toilet seat so they wouldn't leak if the sea came in.

STAN
George Thomson

The waves crashed against the shoreline as Stan sat alone on the desolate beach, his mind unraveling like the threads of a worn-out tapestry. It had been a year since that fateful day when something inside him had snapped, and now he was lost in a world of silence and torment. The sun, high in the sky, seemed to mock him, casting its warm rays upon his vacant stare.

His wife, Sarah, had searched frantically for him after he disappeared that morning. She had combed the beach, shouting his name, her heart pounding in her chest. And then, like a miracle, she found him, sitting motionless, his eyes vacant, a shell of the man he used to be.

In a panic, she rushed him to the hospital, desperate for answers. The doctors conducted numerous tests, hoping to uncover the cause of Stan's sudden mutism. Yet, despite their best efforts, the mystery remained unsolved. Stan could no longer speak, unable to communicate the horrors that had taken hold of his mind.

Days turned into weeks, and weeks into months, as Stan languished in the hospital ward. Sarah visited every day, her love and devotion unwavering, even in the face of the unknown. She would sit by his side, holding his hand, searching his eyes for any sign of recognition. But all she found was an empty abyss, a void where her husband's spirit had once resided.

Ten long years passed, and the memories of that day on the beach had faded into the depths of everyone's minds. Life had moved on, but for the remnants of Stan's family, a shadow hung over their lives. They had come to accept that Stan would never return to them, that the man they once knew was lost forever.

One sunny afternoon, as Sarah and their ten-year-old daughter Jenny strolled along the same beach where their lives had been shattered, fate intervened. Jenny, always curious, wandered off from her mother's side and ventured into a nearby cave. The darkness swallowed her, but she pressed forward, her little heart pounding with excitement and trepidation.

As she explored the damp recesses of the cave, her small hand brushed against something crumpled and forgotten.

Curiosity piqued, she unraveled the note, her eyes widening as she read the words scrawled upon its worn surface. She ran out of the cave and thrust the note into her mothers hands.

The note revealed the unspeakable horrors that had unfolded that day on the beach, the unspeakable horrors that had shattered Stan's mind. Tears streamed down Sarah's face as she read the words, her hands trembling with a mix of disbelief and grief. The weight of the truth bore down on her, threatening to consume her whole.

Returning home, Sarah confronted the agonising revelation with her family. They huddled together in a room heavy with sorrow, the walls closing in on their shared pain. The note spoke of a dark secret, a trauma so profound that it fractured Stan's soul, leaving him trapped within the prison of his own mind.

The truth was unbearable, ripping apart the remnants of their shattered lives. Stan's family, devastated by the revelation, made a solemn vow that day. They would never visit him again, unable to bear the weight of the truth that lay between them. Each day thereafter, their love for Stan remained, but it was a love tinged with anguish, forever tainted by the horrors they had come to know.

Years rolled by, the seasons changing with relentless indifference. Stan, trapped in his own mind, spent his days in the hospital, his existence a mere echo of the vibrant life he had once led. And as time marched on, his family faded from his thoughts, their faces becoming distant and indistinguishable.

Stan's mind had retreated into the darkest corners of his memories, forever entangled with the secrets that had shattered his soul. His days were marked by emptiness, his nights haunted by visions he could never articulate. And as the years slipped away, Stan became a forgotten fragment of a life once lived.

In the end, the silence swallowed him whole, leaving behind only whispers of the truth that lay buried within the depths of that crumpled note.

CHAPTER TWO

The writing prompt for the four stories included in this chapter was simply 'circle'...

THE MAYPOLE
George Thomson

In the year 2053, the world had become a desolate place, trapped within the confines of its own fear. Neglected and forgotten, the maypole stood as a silent witness to the absence of joy. Draped in tattered ribbons that once held the laughter and merriment of a vibrant community, it now stood as a relic of a distant memory.

For three long decades, the villagers had secluded themselves within the confines of their homes and gardens. The outside world had become a ghostly apparition, with no towns bustling with shops, no cinemas, and no restaurants. The very essence of human connection had been reduced to screens and digital interfaces. Dating had become an online affair, where conversations bloomed through the virtual realms of Zoom, Face-time, and similar platforms.

Barry and Colin, two souls yearning for something more, had grown tired of their confined existence. They had spent endless hours chatting online, their conversations an escape from the desolation of their lives. Over time, their connection had deepened, and they knew it was time to take their relationship beyond the realm of digital illusions.

They dared to defy the warnings, to challenge the suffocating fear that held their community hostage. Packing up their belongings, they ventured outside their homes, ready to embark on a journey that would forever change their lives.

As Barry and Colin approached the maypole, a glimmer of hope flickered in their eyes. They took a seat on the ground, facing each other, the neglected ribbons swaying gently in the breeze. In the silence, they could almost hear the echoes of the past, the distant melodies of laughter and the carefree footsteps of dancing villagers.

Their hands touched, and in that simple gesture, they realised the power of human connection. It was a reminder of what had been lost, and what could be reclaimed. With courage as their guide, they vowed to become beacons of change.

News of their defiance spread through the whispers of the wind. It reached the ears of those who had long forgotten the taste of freedom. Slowly but surely, others found the courage to step outside their own homes, to face the world they had abandoned. The tattered ribbons of the maypole became a symbol of resilience, a testament to the human spirit's indomitable nature.

In the days that followed, the village began to awaken from its slumber. People emerged from their self-imposed exiles, their faces yearning for the vibrant colours of life. Together, they danced around the maypole, their smiles a reflection of newfound hope.

Word of their bravery reached neighbouring communities, and a ripple of change spread throughout the land. The chains of fear were shattered, replaced by a yearning for connection and a thirst for the beauty of the world outside.

Towns were rebuilt, shops reopened, and laughter once again echoed through the streets. Cinemas came to life, showcasing stories that reminded people of the importance of human connection. Restaurants bustled with the aroma of shared meals and the joy of breaking bread together.

Nature reclaimed its place in people's lives. Gardens flourished, parks teemed with children's laughter, and the air was filled with the scent of freshly bloomed flowers. The world had rediscovered the beauty it had long forgotten.

As the years passed, the story of Barry and Colin became a legend, a tale of two individuals whose courage had sparked a revolution of the human spirit. Love, trust, and hope flourished once more, and the maypole, now adorned with vibrant ribbons, became a symbol of unity and the resilience of the human heart.

And so, as the world basked in the vibrant colours of life, the once-neglected maypole stood tall, a testament to the power of two souls who dared to defy and brought the world back to the embrace of happiness and connection.

THE CIRCLE
April Berry

I have loved my life; it has been a happy and fulfilling one, filled with pleasurable moments. Oh, don't get me wrong, there have been downs as well as ups, but with Val by my side, there has always been a way to resolve problems and sort out issues, a bit like the Rudyard Kipling poem that is emblazoned above the players' exit at Wimbledon.

As I reminisce back through my life, I find myself smiling. I do a lot of that these days. There's not much else I can do at my age, really. Each day, I take myself back to a part of my life and reflect on what I have done.

As a youngster, I used to spend a lot of time outdoors. I loved the summers—walks into the nearby woods, playing in the stream, swinging on the tire swing that hung from a large sycamore tree by the bank of the stream. I would make my way home when dusk started to set in. I had a brilliant childhood; I wanted for nothing. My parents were very loving and supportive.

In those days, we didn't have electronic devices. In fact, not all homes had a telephone. Another memory that brings a smile to my face. We had a party line at home, which meant we shared it with a neighbour. It was annoying when I wanted to call my friends and the neighbours were on the phone. You could hear the click as the other party picked up the phone. I'm sure they used to stay on the phone longer just to spite me, well, that's what I told myself. And to make matters worse, the wife was one of my teachers at school. I am positive that she used to punish me in school for things she overheard me say on the phone!

Other memories I like to dwell on are when I got married. Val looked beautiful walking down the aisle; I was the happiest man alive. Pride made my chest swell, though I did let a small tear roll down my face; tears of unbridled happiness, I hasten to add.

We went on to have three lovely children. They were not perfect by any means, especially Gary, who, in his teens, was brought home more nights by the local bobby than I care to think about. Constable Evans was a lovely bloke, and I knew he could see the good in Gary despite the mischief he got up to. Gary, along with his two sisters, is now married with children of his own. Oh, the joy they brought to Val and me. She was always volunteering to babysit. Most weekends, we had a house full—laughter, noise, and tears never ceasing. All the cousins were close, and so were our children and their partners.

I remember one family holiday to Tenby—there were 15 of us, with all the children, spouses, and grandchildren. We had a fabulous time.

Life moves on, though, and now the grandchildren have partners. I often wonder what happened to the institution of marriage, as none of the grandchildren are married, but some do live with their partners. Gary's eldest is with someone of the same sex. I really worried at first, knowing how bad it was back in the day for same-sex couples, but they reassure me that it's not an issue now and they can marry if they wish.

I had a wonderful job with a really good boss. I was treated with respect at work, worked my way up in the firm, and left with a good pension. You could even say my life was nothing remarkable—average, really—but to me, I was as happy as a pig in muck!

I was able to retire early, and Val and I fulfilled all the trips we had dreamed of—Hawaii, Rio, Las Vegas, Sydney, a few romantic trips to Paris. They were possibly the highlights of my retirement.

Val and I were soulmates in every sense of the word, and the bottom dropped out of my life when Val died. She was ill for a while, but ever the optimist, I thought she would pull through. No amount of sympathy and love from our children could console me.

Eventually, life started to resemble something resembling normality. Oh, don't get me wrong, I missed Val tremendously, but I started to check off the items on our bucket list, sitting at night with a small whiskey, filling Val in on what I had done that day.

One day, while walking along the Jurassic trail, I noticed an ache in my legs I had never felt before. That was the start of my downward spiral health-wise. Visits to the hospital and the doctors, all the treatments and prescriptions, didn't stop this hideous illness from taking over my body, eventually rendering me practically helpless. It was my worst nightmare. I had always hoped that I would lose my mind, not my physical abilities, but it was not to be. My mind is razor-sharp, and I have the body of a very large baby, in the care of the local nursing home, living my life now through the memories I made throughout my life.

I came into the world as a helpless baby, and I am leaving it in the same state. Well, I guess that's the circle of life.

TRANS CENTRIC CIRCLES
Daizi Rae

Eloise laughs at her own clumsiness as she throws yet another ring that misses the mark on the Ring Toss stall at the Goose Fair in Nottingham. She's having the best night, coming to the fair as a second date with Dylan was such a good idea.

Dylans sense of humour matched Eloise to perfection and he was already planning their third date in his head, he thought they were made for each other. He just loved a girl that could laugh at herself, she seemed to embrace life in all the little things. They leave the Ring Toss stall with giggle and a sad little bear of a consolation prize that will probably live its life in a decoupaged box of happy memories in the back of a wardrobe somewhere.

Eloise and Dylan are walking arm in arm when they hear shouting and sobs just ahead of them. 'What the hell…' mutters Eloise as they come across a girl in tears, being picked on while everyone just walks past her, too embarrassed or too afraid to help, or they just didn't care enough to take it seriously, not their business, right!

'What are you anyway, your not a real girl!' This from a skinny little runt of a lad, sniggering to his mates who were yelling and whooping as they circled the innocent young girl who was now the miserable and frightened object of their taunts.

'Yeah,' yelled his mate, 'we don't need you trannys at our fair. Bugger off home, you don't belong here.'

'It's a she-male,' laughed the third of the circling lads, joining in, desperate to be accepted as one of the 'the lads.'

Eloises eyes widen in horror at the disgraceful behaviour she was witnessing and without another thought she stepped up to the circle…

'Oi! What the hell are you doing, leave her alone!' She said, as Dylan stepped up beside her and took her hand.

'Be careful,' he whispered. We don't want to be in the middle of that circle with her.'

The runt turned towards Eloise and Dylan, and a grin lit up his rat like little face - 'Oh, look lads, it must be a full moon or summat, there's more of em.'

The laughter from the lads started drying up when Eloise stepped up to the leader of the tormentors and took his full attention, to say: 'You know everyone has a right to be here and have a good time without you being all up in their face, right?'

'OOOh did he/she say something,' he smirked, looking to his friends for support, only to find them looking at the floor, uncomfortably avoiding his gaze. He turned back looking a little less sure of himself now the numbers had evened up. Having no idea how to 'read the room' he turned back to Eloise ready to spit his next little gem of ignorant poison.

Meanwhile, Dylan slipped behind the boys while they were preoccupied with Eloise and grabbed the girls hand and pulled her out of the circle and harms way.

Eloise gave the leader a second to become aware that the tide had turned and his circle of torment was empty, before saying, 'Are you sure you want to carry this on, theres three of you and three of us now?'

Apparently this little skirmish wasn't going unnoticed or ignored any longer, as a chap stepped up next to Dylan and said, 'Make that four of us.'

'Five,' came another voice.

'Six,' said yet another.

Eloise and Dylan turned to look at the people who had chosen to stand with them, and the three would be tormentors took their chance and skulked off, knowing they were out of their depth and not wanting to be in the centre of any circle themselves. It's too easy to judge other people by your own standards, so it didn't occur to them to consider any other outcome.

'Thank you,' Eloise said to their sudden allies.

'Think nothing of it,' said number four, dropping Eloise a wink. 'Enjoy the rest of your evening. Don't give those guys another thought,' he said as he melted back into the crowd.

'Thank you for rescuing me,' said the girl, smiling. 'I'm Julie, and I was proper scared there for a while.'

'Hi Julie, nice to meet you, I'm Dylan, this is Eloise. Why don't you join us?

'And don't think anything of it,' said Eloise. 'We wouldn't leave anyone to suffer that kind of ignorant bullying. Look, I can see the Hook-a-Duck stand, come on, who fancies their chances at winning one of those massive unicorns!'

Dylan smiled to himself, thinking he may just have fallen a little bit in love with his beautiful brave date.

THE CIRCLES OF LIFE
Gerry O'Keeffe

A circle is a wonderful thing. It comes in various sizes and forms, often taken for granted. Our breakfast bowl, considered by some (and I fully agree), is the most important meal to start the day, and it is often circular. The sun that awakens us in the morning is circular. Most of the plates we use for meals, which sustain our lives, are also circular. When humans first invented the wheel, did they realise how much it would forever change our lives for the better?

Ted lay in his bed, gazing out of his round window. Contemplating these thoughts, he looked at one of his favourite things in the entire universe: the moon. Ted wondered if the moon might even be greater than the sun because he could safely observe it through his beautiful circular window without the fear of going blind. However, the truly greatest circular thing that he could do wonderful things with was a football. With the full moon shining tonight, Ted held the football up to cover the moon, and it fit perfectly. The football seemed to say, "Yes, Ted, I am as great as, or perhaps even better than, the moon."

However, something unexpected began to appear, which would likely change Ted's entire perspective. Similar to the invention of the wheel, this would alter his life forever. A gold sparkly light emerged, swirling in a circular shape and creating a small hole. Through this hole, an arm appeared, holding a permanent marker pen. The arm extended towards the ball and beckoned Ted to bring it closer to be signed. Ted, astonished, followed the finger's suggestion, moving the ball for the floating arm to sign it. First, it wrote the number 10, then inside the zero, "for the magic we create," and finally, it signed its name with just four letters—the four greatest letters in the history of football. This player was Ted's favourite in the whole universe, the first one he ever collected in his sticker collection book. The player he aspired to play and be like, just as the wheel changed the world forever.

As Ted observed this extraordinary event, he was even more amazed when the hand waved at him and then, as if in slow motion, disappeared through the golden sparkly hole. However, within seconds, the same index finger reappeared. This time, it traced the tip around the hole, making it bigger and bigger until it was large enough for someone to pass through. The finger once again beckoned Ted to enter. Ted pointed at his own chest, as if to ask, "Me?" Still in disbelief that this was happening, especially to him, who never felt deserving of anything good. No one had ever viewed him as such, until now. Ted, summoned by the greatest footballer to have ever lived, was being called to a whole new world. If this was a dream, it was the greatest one of all time.

Ted slowly got up and stumbled towards the enormous circle in the middle of his bedroom. First, he stuck his head through and saw a beautifully manicured green pitch with players from different eras scattered across it, all wearing the number 10 on their backs and shorts. Excitedly, Ted stepped through the magical circle and was greeted by a deafening roar of noise, with the crowd screaming his name: "We want Ted, we want Ted!" His crutches, which he relied on, vanished, and for the first time in his life, he felt strength in his legs. Looking down, he saw he was wearing football boots. His eyes followed up his body, revealing that he was donned in a full football kit, proudly displaying the number 10.

Glancing towards the stands, Ted spotted an enormous silver and gold trophy awaiting the winners. He pinched himself hard to verify if he was dreaming, and the sensation of pain confirmed that this was indeed real. Something that would be further confirmed by the relentless tackles he received during the game of his life, culminating in a harsh challenge from a rival number 10. The foul was committed in the box, resulting in a penalty kick in the 119th minute with the score tied at 9 all. Ted had already scored four goals, while his favourite number 10 had five. After gingerly rising from the tackle, he was handed the ball. Placing it down, his heart raced faster than a speeding bullet. Taking a few steps back, he shifted his eyes, sending the goalkeeper the wrong way and calmly rolled the ball into the net on the other side. The crowd erupted in wild celebration, with Ted's teammates joyfully piling on top of him. Moments later, the final whistle blew, marking the end of the game. The pitch became a scene of exuberant jubilation, filled with singing, dancing, handshakes, and commiserations.

When it was time to receive the trophy, which was circular like a football with prominent ears, Ted was handed the coveted prize. "Go on, you deserve it. Enjoy," they said. As the same sparkly portal circle began to form again, Ted bid farewell to his new wonderful friends, waving at them as he passed through. Exhausted, he collapsed onto his bed and fell fast asleep.

"Wow! That dream last night was something," Ted thought upon waking up. His eyes were momentarily blinded by the gleaming trophy lying beside him. He hugged it tightly, beaming with delight, and exclaimed, "Circles truly are the greatest things in my life. EVER!"

CHAPTER THREE

We gave out the writing prompt of 'Cliche' for this chapter...

SALT OF THE EARTH
Sandy Biddles

Father and son stood in front of the kitchen window on Lytton Street, smiling for the camera. Arthur had his arm around the shoulders of a short, stocky man in a flat cap and braces, who stood proudly with folded arms. Both had lived through one war, with another just around the corner.

Albert's own father had worked as a miner at Radford Colliery, and his sons followed him down the pit. After hell broke loose in 1914, coal became as essential to Britain's victory as men going into combat. While some of the younger pit-men enlisted, those with wives and families to support stayed in the pit.

Arthur was a baby then, with older siblings and more to follow. His childhood taught him to be resourceful. Finding an old wooden barrow at the nearby dump, he door-knocked for metal scrap to sell in exchange for odd jobs and errands, while avoiding the local rag 'n bone man on his cart, who would give him a clip round the ear, or worse.

Not for nothing was the colliery known as the Bread and Herring Pit. It may be a cliché, but life was hard. The street-smart, funny, bright young man embracing his father had, like his brothers, started working at the mine at 15, soon moving to the coalface, with black dust and earth seeping into his blood. His elder sister, Ada, was one of the pit-brow girls, picking dirt and stones from the freshly mined coal. They would start their day at 6 am, wearing wooden clogs to protect their feet from the pile of debris, which was only cleared at the end of the day.

Arthur had amassed some Raleigh bicycle parts in the backyard, much to his mother's annoyance when pegging out the sheets or airing Duggie, the latest baby, in his perambulator. So, while not at the pit and not yet old enough to join his dad at the pub, he soon assembled a rudimentary bike for himself and repaired others for a few bob once the word had spread among the neighbours.

It was around this time (Arthur couldn't recall the exact date) when Albert had an accident. An insecure roof prop, thickly obscured by coal dust, had gone unnoticed. He was lucky, suffering a nasty head wound and a short spell in Nottingham General Hospital, covered by his insurance. Kathleen claimed it must have knocked some sense into him or sent him doolally, though she never made up her mind on the subject.

At any rate, after much discussion and late-night mutterings in the parlour, the couple decided to rent a nearby shop, live on the premises, and set up a respectable family hardware business.

Spring 1939: Rumblings of instability in Europe, with newspaper headlines whipping up speculation about the prospect of another war. Albert, nearly 60, was too old to be conscripted, but Kathleen lived in daily fear for her son's safety. By now, Ada was married and Clarice was engaged. Then, on 3rd September, the unthinkable happened as Britain declared war on Germany.

Kathleen's fears were realised as her elder boys were immediately conscripted. They sent Arthur to Ossett, amidst the Yorkshire pits, for military training, making him a signaller and posting him to France in the early 1940s. I know this because he later sang me songs of resistance and heroism.

He never talked about experiencing the French earth under fire or bombardment, but I can picture him riding his Raleigh bicycle, dispatching messages between encampments. My dad: a proud man, salt of the earth, like his father, and his father before him.

UPHILL BATTLE
J A Fabre

I spent most of today sitting on my couch, indulging in a "Glitch" marathon on Netflix. For dinner, I treated myself to some delicious Chinese food—chicken and mushroom with special fried rice, prawn toast, and seaweed. I must admit, I enjoyed a hearty plateful, even though I remained glued to the sofa for the rest of the night. It wasn't until 1:30 am that I finally decided to call it a night. Surprisingly, at 4:30 am, I find myself wide awake, my body still adjusting to the generous amount of food I consumed. What was I thinking? The other half of my meal sits in the fridge, tempting me for tomorrow. But you know what? I have a plan. I'll have it as an earlier meal and make it my only indulgence of the day. That way, it's a step in the right direction, isn't it? Maybe it's time for a change.

As I sit here in the dark, unable to sleep, I reflect on my actions. I've been overeating for what feels like an eternity, but tonight, something feels different. I'm being brutally honest with myself, baring my soul without any fear of judgment. This dark moment might just be the turning point I've been longing for.

Let's talk about body image. The reflection staring back at me in the mirror no longer fills me with disgust alone. It's also accompanied by a spark of determination. As I step out of the shower and catch a glimpse of my reflection, I feel a flicker of motivation deep within me. Yes, there's work to be done, but there's also the potential for transformation. That gut I see can be conquered, and that flabby excess can be sculpted into strength. I remember the days when a chiseled jawline and confidence defined me. I yearn to reclaim that version of myself.

Right now, I might be at the lowest point mentally and physically, but I refuse to accept defeat. I know I hold the power to change my circumstances. I'm aware of the steps needed for improvement - eating healthier, exercising regularly, and hydrating my body. It's not an insurmountable challenge; it's a journey to self-discovery and self-care.

This is my wake-up call, my realisation that I deserve better. I'm ready to embark on this path of transformation, even if it's challenging. I no longer wish to suffer in silence or hope for someone to save me. Instead, I'm taking control of my life, seeking the strength within myself to rise above this self-destructive cycle.

So here I am, sharing my story, a declaration of vulnerability and determination. I know there will be obstacles along the way, but I'm optimistic that I can overcome them. This is my plea for support, not because I can't do it alone, but because we all thrive with encouragement and guidance.

If you're reading this, know that I'm ready to embrace change, ready to become the best version of myself. Together, let's embark on this journey—one filled with self-discovery, growth, and ultimately, a triumph over the darkness that has plagued me for far too long. I believe in myself, and I'm excited to see what lies ahead.

IT WASN'T ME
Jayne Love

Back in the '60s and '70s, if people found out you lived in a children's home, they automatically thought the court had sent you or your parents had because you had been so naughty, you had to live away from a normal upbringing.

I wasn't a good or easy child, but I had my reasons, best kept to myself. My mother had died and had never named my dad, so I wound up in care. Don't get me wrong, there were one or two kids in our home that a court had sent, but it was not the norm.

There were twenty kids aged from 6 to 18 back then, but we got on reasonably well. We watched out for each other inside and outside the home. Mostly, the staff were okay with us, except the superintendent, Uncle Len. He was a tyrant, a control freak, and he got that control anyway he could, physically or mentally.

He would do fire drills at 2 am randomly. If we failed to get up and out in 5 minutes, he told us he would repeat the exercise until we got it right. However, he wouldn't say when. So the older kids tried to stay awake to give us a head start. The alarm didn't always go off that night, but the next and the next. One week it happened every night. We went to school totally drained.

One day, as I walked in from school, I sensed a grim atmosphere. This usually meant they had caught someone doing something wrong. We were all in for the aftermath of Uncle Len's anger.

I was told to go straight to the office, which I did, racking my brain going through all I had done lately, trying to think what I could've done wrong to get into trouble.

There was a police officer sitting in one chair, and Uncle Len sat in another. "A woman was attacked and robbed on Grey Street at about ten past four yesterday afternoon. You were seen on Grey Street about that time," the officer said.

"I'm not sure of the time, but I get off the bus and walk down Grey Street to cut down the ginnel every day from school," I replied.

"Known as a fighter, aren't you Kate? Bit of a hard case?" the officer said.

"Just schoolyard scuffles," I replied, looking at my shoes.

"Face the officer when you speak to him," ordered Uncle Len.

"Did you see anything or anyone on your walk home?" the officer said.

"No," I replied.

I asked if this girl was in uniform, as I wore a different uniform than most of the girls who lived in or near the children's home. I attended high school, and most others went to the local comprehensive. He didn't answer me. I was just told to wait outside while they discussed what would happen next.

I was to be taken to the police station and questioned. "An adult will be required to accompany her," I heard him say.

They took me to the station, put me in a room with a female officer. No one spoke to me except to say, "Sit down." They left me there until my social worker, Miss Jones, arrived, and they asked me the same questions as before, and I gave the same answers.

It seemed like hours I was in there, then they eventually said I could go home. I heard nothing for nearly two weeks until Uncle Len informed me that a girl had been arrested. I was in the clear. No apology for what I'd been through. I looked at him and said defiantly, "Told you it wasn't me."

FATE
Daizi Rae

Jenny walked along The Promenade, twirling her umbrella in the rain and humming to herself. She was on her way home from her last ever shift at the Bluebird Bar, and she was in the best mood she had been in for weeks. No more night shifts serving sleazy, drunken punters, thinking copping a feel every time she cleared their table was all part of the service. No more sticky floors, never again having to wear that ridiculous, degrading uniform that left nothing to the imagination. Jenny believed in the philosophy that life significantly changed every seven years. And here she was, on the cusp of substantial change, right on cue. It was written in the stars. This was her time.

~

Georgia, like every other night, had been sitting at her usual table in the bar. She was certain she was just another face, in another dark corner of this shabby place. She was a broken woman. For two months, she had been sitting at the same table, having her drinks served to her by her love, her obsession, her everything—Jenny, if only she had known. There were nights when she thought she saw a flicker in Jenny's eyes as she looked at her, but many more nights when she was certain that it was not true. Tonight was just another night she was blind to the tears winding their way down Georgia's cheek. The tears added to the dark patch that was slowly spreading along her shirt collar, representing the agony of being so near to Jenny for the last time.

~

Jenny was smiling to herself, but she had one small regret. Not enough to make her stay at the Bluebird. Hell no, she was glad to be out of there. But there was that woman. She had the kindest eyes. She was a regular, always took the same table, and was always alone. Something inside Jenny always felt special whenever she looked at her. Yet they had never had a conversation outside of Jenny serving her drinks and flashing what she hoped was her most engaging smile. But obviously, she was invisible to her, and now it was too late. Some things are just not meant to be. She couldn't believe in fate and destiny and seven-year cycles and not take it as an omen of a relationship that was just not meant to be. Two months of seeing one another every single time Jenny had ever been on shift, and nothing, not a word.

~

Georgia shrugged into her jacket and left the bar for the last time. There was no need to ever come back now, was there? She turned along The Promenade and headed towards home, kicking herself for her crippling shyness. She was thinking about all the things she should have said to Jenny when her quiet reflections were shattered by the sound of a scream just ahead of her. She stopped dead in her tracks and listened. For a moment, there was nothing, and she thought maybe she had imagined it. Then she heard a frightened sob followed by a plea of "please don't hurt me."

Moving purely on instinct, Georgia approached the source of the scream. She saw a group of men surrounding a young woman, their intentions clear. Without hesitation, she rushed towards them, yelling and making as much noise as possible. The men turned to face her, momentarily startled, and Georgia used the opportunity to pull the frightened woman away from them. She quickly assessed the situation and realised that they were outnumbered and outmatched, but she refused to back down. With fierce determination, she stood her ground and held the woman behind her, shielding her from harm.

~

As luck would have it, Jenny was still on The Promenade. She heard the commotion and recognised Georgia's voice. She rushed towards the sound of the struggle and saw Georgia bravely standing up to the group of men. Jenny didn't hesitate for a moment and joined in the fight, throwing punches and kicks with surprising agility. Together, Jenny and Georgia managed to fight off the attackers, sending them running in all directions. The two women hugged each other, both relieved and exhilarated by their unexpected victory. They walked the young woman home, making sure she was safe and looked after. Before they went their separate ways, they exchanged numbers, promising to meet up soon. As each of them walked towards her own home, Jenny realised that fate had brought them together for a reason. She felt grateful for the opportunity to get to know Georgia better and excited to see where this new friendship would lead.

They say silence speaks volumes, but that is clearly not always the case.

CHAPTER FOUR

'Sorry, not sorry!' We've all heard that one right. Lots of us have done things in our lives that we fully justify, good or bad. So that was where the writing prompt for this chapter came from. Unrepentant...

GIP
Finbar Ansbe

Once upon a time, there was a pig named Gip. Gip was one cool motherfucking pig. This motherfucker had it all. They were in a band, a successful one. Their first album, "Brick House," was widely renowned as a cult classic. The band had called themselves The Three Little Pigs; it was funny because there were four of them. And also, it was funny because they were all at least 6ft tall, and Gaston, their drummer, was 6ft 7. Gip was the bassist but also sang and wrote all the lyrics. Paul McCartney, Kate Nash, and Thundercat were all particular inspirations of Gip's. Gip rode a motorcycle; her name was Shelly. Gip was also a great gardener; their allotment was filled to the rims with beautifully vivid vegetables of all colours: bright red tomatoes, crunchy orange carrots, succulent green cucumbers, pink and purple radishes, all the size of your head. Gip gave great advice, was excellent at Sudoku, and was always out and about helping the community: food banks, youth clubs, you name it. Friends would often say things to Gip like, "Yo Gip! Damn, you're a good motorcycle rider!" or "Wow Gip! That was one impressive backflip!" All the praise was a lot for Gip sometimes, but still, they never forgot to say thank you.

However, Gip had a secret.

One day in the deep of summer, cracks of sunshine broke through the blinds and awoke Gip, nice and early. They felt a bit rough, but it was nothing that a cold shower and a microwaved portion of last night's supper couldn't fix – Gip always ate the same meal. They read the morning newspaper and then, at around 11 am, hopped on Shelly and made their way down to the beach.

Once Gip had arrived, they parked up their trusty bike, grabbed their trendy beach bag, and went to find a spot. They liked to position themselves middle-ish, not too far from Shelly, but at the same time not too far from the sea. They pulled their book, "Outliers" by Malcolm Gladwell, out of that quirky beach bag of theirs, put on their shades, and began to relax. Gip spent the whole day there, occasionally nipping into the water for a quick dip; they were an excellent swimmer, of course. As the sun made its way from east to west, they saw all arrays of day-trippers come and go: the dog walkers, the families, the sweet but obnoxious students who were drinking, dancing, and seeming to stay a little longer than everyone else.

But eventually, the students left too. Gip waited half an hour after everyone was gone before they made their move, just to be sure. Then, when that timer went off on their phone, just like clockwork, they packed their stuff back into their unnecessarily fashionable beach bag and headed back up to Shelly. Carefully, Gip slipped the beach bag back into Shelly's saddlebag and retrieved a different bag – a small brown tote bag. They placed this bag around their shoulder; this bag was somehow even trendier than the first one. Then they gave Shelly a little kiss on her handles and trotted back down to the beach. But when Gip arrived at the beach, they kept trotting. Round the corner they went, over the bridge, and slowly, into the woods. One hoof at a time, they meandered through the trees, making sure not to step on any twigs or sticks that looked especially crunchy. With the grace and dexterity of a ballerina, they slid up and down boulders, hopped over passing streams, and ducked under pokey bushes. When Gip arrived at their usual spot, they climbed nimbly up that familiar tree. They always sat on the same, long, sturdy branch, as this branch, without a doubt, was the best one for pigs to sit on in occasions such as these. Entirely focused on the job at hand now, Gip pulled out their trusty Barrett M82. And then, as routinely as one may brush their teeth, make a coffee, or butter some toast: BANG!

Gip, as you can probably imagine, was a superb sniper. They carefully repacked Barrett into their nifty little tote bag and made their way back down the tree. Then, humming a little tune as they went, Gip popped their supper over their back and headed back to the car park. On arrival, they whipped out a bin bag from Shelly's saddlebag, wrapped the wolf up, and duct-taped it onto the back of their loyal vehicle.

You see, everyone knows the story of The Three Little Pigs. Everyone's heard all about how, eventually, the final little pig outsmarted the big bad wolf, capturing him in a big pot of boiling water and eating him for supper. But what everyone conveniently doesn't know about the story of The Three Little

Pigs is that the final little pig had a pregnant wife and that the final little pig spent the rest of his life behind bars, and that the final little pig's son grew up without a father.

Every time they loaded a wolf onto Shelly's back, Gip thought of their great-grandfather; how proud he'd be! And on this particular summer's night, Gip glided round those familiar winding roads, as they so often did, thinking about the violent system that had forced them to take justice into their own hands. Pirouetting through the mountains, Gip's mind's eye was filled with all the wolves unfairly protected, all the lives lost, and all the little pigs growing up without fathers. But as they pulled up into their drive and carefully undid the duct tape that had expertly harnessed that bastard onto Shelly, as they used their abnormal strength to carry their latest spot of revenge inside, as they slid their scrumptious snack into their trusty pan and admired its water's sterile simmer grow to an elegant boil, Gip felt calm.

Alexa! Play "The Last Laugh" by The Three Little Pigs.

UNREPENTANT
April Berry

Crouching behind a grassy hummock, I looked around the landscape, squinting in the mid-morning sun. I knew what I was looking for, but I just couldn't see it. How did I end up here? A 23-year-old woman, supposed to be in my final year of medical studies, yet here I was, 30 miles from the nearest town. A desolate beach lay to my left, with grassy dunes and shrub land to my right. I glanced at my watch, tutting as loudly as I dared. Every second counted; it could be the difference between life and death.

Allowing myself a rare moment of nostalgia, I thought back to four years ago when I was carefree, late for everything, and nonchalantly shrugging off people's comments about my timekeeping. Now it was the most important thing in my life.

Hearing a rustle to my right, my senses heightened. I turnèd my head and could see the grass moving, like a snake through the desert. As the rustling came closer, I could make out two grey figures crawling forward in the grass.

As they got closer, something told me things were off. There were only supposed to be two, but I could make out a third body in the grass. I needed to escape! Acting fast, I turned to run parallel to the beach. But in my haste, I got my coat belt tangled in the handlebars of my bike, which came crashing down on top of me.

Looking up, I could see three figures standing in front of me. A British pilot with a bloody nose, swollen eye socket, and visible bruises all over his face was flanked by two slightly disheveled Gestapo officers. In that moment, I knew we had been betrayed. Panicked thoughts clouded my mind. Had all our covers been blown? Would all members of the resistance cell be arrested? I knew that what followed wouldn't be pleasant, but I had been trained for this. If I'm honest, I was terrified in that moment. Adrenaline coursed through my veins, and after what was only a few seconds, I stood up straight to face my fate.

The British pilot and I were dragged across the sand dunes to the road and thrown into the back of a windowless van that reeked of a cattle barn. No doubt the previous occupants, knowing their fate, had soiled themselves, and no one had bothered to clean it out.

The vehicle stopped, and we were dragged out of the van, pulled down multiple corridors, and pushed downstairs. Eventually, we were split up, and I was violently pushed into a cell.

The cell was damp, freezing, and the only light came from a bare bulb suspended from the ceiling.

I sat down on the floor and took stock of my situation.

Thinking back two years when I joined the resistance, I knew the dangers, but my successes along the way had far outweighed the possibility of being caught. Also, at 23, I thought I was invincible. However, now I knew I was on my way to meet my maker. I felt strangely calm, very peaceful. All the successful repatriations I had accomplished seemed to give me comfort for the situation I now found myself in. All those young men who had made it back to their families.

My questioning went on for what seemed like weeks. Gentle persuasion followed by brutal beatings, but nothing they did to me would make me give up the transport smuggling lines for the repatriation of allied forces. I knew the pilot was no use to them and was afraid that they would kill him. But I couldn't be too concerned, as that would bring my guard down, and I might slip up.

I became quite good at counting time in my head, though it may not have been truly accurate. It felt like I was left alone for a while, and I could feel the lacerations and bruises on my face heal. My body also started to repair from the beatings. I did wonder why. Maybe they realised that I was never going to be broken.

I heard boots coming down the corridor, keys in the lock, and my cell door swung open. I was grabbed by both arms and pulled out of my cell, but this time we turned a different way than when I was being interrogated. I felt a lump in my throat as I knew what was coming. I was being transported to the concentration camps.

The light of the courtyard blinded me. It was the first time I had seen daylight since the day on the sand dunes. I struggled to focus as we moved across the courtyard, like some clumsy three-legged race, and stopped in front of a wall.

As my eyesight came back to me, I could see that I wasn't being transported. In front of me was a line of people, all holding rifles, and they were pointed at me. I felt the sweat trickle down the back of my neck. I went cold all over, and the initial terror was nearly more than I could bear.

I closed my eyes, waiting for the shots to ring out. A strange calmness washed over me.

DARK PLEASURES
George Thomson

Karen sat at her desk in the dimly lit typing pool, surrounded by the monotonous clacking of typewriters. Five other women worked alongside her, their faces etched with weariness and resignation. But Karen was different. She harboured a secret pleasure, a dark joy that fuelled her every action.

During her breaks, Karen would retreat to a small corner of the office, hidden from prying eyes. There, with a wicked grin on her face, she would craft poison pen letters. Her colleagues were her unwitting targets, unsuspecting victims of her malevolence. The letters were filled with biting words, cruel insinuations, and malicious falsehoods. Karen took immense pleasure in writing the nastiest things she could conjure.

She relished in the power she held over her coworkers. The bitterness in the letters was seldom true, but that made it all the more exhilarating fo Karen. She delighted in inflicting hurt and misery on these unsuspecting women. And the icing on the cake was the chance to witness their devastation firsthand.

Karen would nonchalantly join her colleagues as they gathered to open their mail, concealing her true intentions. She would console them, feigning sympathy as they read the venomous words that spilled from the pages. It was her front-row seat to watch the results of her actions, the culmination of her twisted art. And she was never even the slightest bit sorry.

The office was slowly being consumed by an atmosphere of paranoia and suspicion. The women turned against each other, whispering, and casting accusing glances. Trust vanished like smoke, leaving behind an unsettling air of tension. Karen revelled in the chaos she had sown, basking in her role as the puppet master of their lives.

Days turned into weeks, and Karen's game continued unabated. The toxicity she created swirled around the office, suffocating those unfortunate enough to be ensnared in its grasp. Yet, none suspected Karen, the seemingly innocent woman who was always there to offer comfort. She revelled in her double life, the darkness simmering beneath her pleasant facade.

But then, one fateful day, an envelope addressed to Karen arrived. A shiver of anticipation ran down her spine as she tore it open, unaware that her game was about to be exposed. The poison pen letter within was unlike any she had crafted. It was filled with the same venom and cruelty, laced with an intimate knowledge of her own darkest secrets.

Karen's heart raced, and a cold sweat formed on her brow. How had her secret been discovered? Panic gripped her, the twisted joy she had once experienced replaced by a gnawing fear. The tables had turned, and she found herself on the receiving end of the very poison she had so gleefully dispensed.

Days turned into sleepless nights as Karen became a prisoner of her own creation. Paranoia took hold, haunting every waking moment. She saw her colleagues' glances, whispers that seemed to echo with accusation. The walls of the office, once suffused with her power, now closed in on her, squeezing the air from her lungs.

No longer did Karen find pleasure in her twisted game. The letters she had sent felt like millstones around her neck, suffocating her spirit. The very misery she had inflicted on others had returned to consume her. And in the darkest corners of her mind, a tiny seed of remorse began to sprout.

One day, unable to bear the weight of her own guilt, Karen mustered the courage to confess her actions. Tears streamed down her face as she admitted to her colleagues the depths of her deceit, the pain she had intentionally caused. Their faces held a mixture of shock, anger, and sadness, but there was also a glimmer of forgiveness.

In the aftermath, Karen faced the consequences of her actions. Her reputation was tarnished, and she became an outcast in the office. But she had learned a harsh lesson—the consequences of inflicting pain and misery on others were not worth the temporary thrill she had once relished. The emptiness she felt inside was a stark reminder of the hollowness of her former pleasure.

Karen vowed to change. She sought therapy, seeking to understand the twisted motivations that had driven her to such dark depths. Slowly, she rebuilt her life, seeking redemption for the harm she had caused. The path was arduous, forgiveness hard-won, but Karen persevered, determined to become a better person.

In the end, Karen emerged from the darkness, a changed woman. The typing pool became a place of healing, where she worked alongside her former victims, united by the scars they carried. And as the clacking of typewriters filled the air, Karen found solace in knowing that she had left her poison pen letters in the past, forever.

Probably!

STAPLEFORD
Daizi Rae

The quaint suburb of Stapleford nestled on the outskirts of Nottingham, was like any other ordinary neighbourhood at first glance. Gossips buzzed through the local pub, drinkers laughed boisterously, and the eclectic mix of weirdos and respectable folk coexisted in an uneasy harmony. But beneath the surface of this seemingly unremarkable town lurked tales of strange happenings that had intrigued many for years.

Caroline Donald, an independent writer with a troubled past, returned to Stapleford to confront her demons and write a novel inspired by her early years. Childhood terrors had haunted her for too long, and she sought solace and closure in her childhood home. Little did she know that the ghosts of her past were not the only ones she would encounter.

Upon her return, Caroline discovered that her childhood home, where she hoped to find comfort, was now rented by a mysterious newcomer. His aura exuded an uncanny allure that sent shivers down Caroline's spine. Although she couldn't put her finger on what made him so unsettling, she couldn't shake the feeling of unease whenever he was around.

As Caroline delved into writing her novel, strange occurrences began to unfold around the town. It started subtly; a child from the neighbourhood disappeared without a trace, leaving the community in a state of despair. The local authorities brushed it off as a mere missing person's case, not uncommon in a suburb like Stapleford. But then, things took a darker turn.

A series of disturbing events began to plague the town—a dog was found brutally killed in a manner too grotesque to be the work of any ordinary predator. Caroline tried to rationalise these events, putting them down to coincidence and the usual mishaps that could befall any neighbourhood. Yet, as the list of unsettling incidents grew, so did her apprehension.

Rumours whispered through the town like an eerie wind. Some claimed that the newcomer was responsible for the misfortunes, while others believed that the supernatural had once again awakened in Stapleford, seeking revenge for forgotten sins. The line between reality and folklore blurred, and fear blanketed the once peaceful streets.

Caroline's writing became an obsession as she attempted to weave together the threads of her past with the ominous present. But the more she explored her memories, the more she realised how unreliable they had become. Were her recollections tainted by fear and trauma? Or was the past being manipulated by an unseen malevolence that now lurked in the shadows of Stapleford?

In her quest for answers, Caroline sought out some of the town's more colourful inhabitants—each with their own secrets and suspicions. Among them, a group of elderly women who huddled together in a coven-like fashion, their eyes filled with both wisdom and fear. They warned Caroline of an ancient curse that had befallen the land long ago, and how it had been awakened by the newcomer's arrival.

Despite her initial skepticism, Caroline couldn't ignore the mounting evidence of inexplicable occurrences. The town seemed to hold its breath, waiting for the next disaster to strike. Nightmares plagued her sleep, and she found herself haunted by visions of shadows moving with sinister intent.

As the town's unrest grew, Caroline's unease deepened. She became determined to uncover the truth, even if it meant facing her deepest fears head-on. She revisited the house she once called home, where the catalyst for her childhood terrors had occurred.

Inside, she found the newcomer, who greeted her with a disconcerting smile. The house seemed to whisper with secrets, and Caroline's heart pounded as she demanded answers from the enigmatic stranger.

He spoke cryptically, hinting at a past that transcended time. A past that tied him to the very essence of Stapleford. He claimed to be more than a mere man, the harbinger of a force older than memory, drawn back to this town like a moth to a flame.

Fear and curiosity warred within Caroline as she struggled to comprehend the truth he unveiled. The newcomer's allure, it seemed, was no mere charm but a magnetic pull - a dark force that drew others into his orbit, a force that craved chaos and despair.

Caroline's mind raced as she grappled with the enormity of what she had stumbled upon. The newcomer had awakened something ancient and malevolent in Stapleford, something that fed off fear and sorrow, and it had chosen her childhood home as its epicentre.

Time seemed to unravel, and the town fell deeper into darkness. The newcomer's true intentions remained veiled, but Caroline knew that stopping him was paramount to saving Stapleford from an unfathomable fate.

With newfound resolve, Caroline embarked on a treacherous journey to thwart the malevolent force and lay her childhood terrors to rest once and for all. She sought allies among the colourful townsfolk, uniting them in a desperate attempt to confront the darkness that had infested their homes.

As the confrontation loomed, the line between surprise, bewilderment, and terror blurred for the residents of Stapleford. The battle that ensued would test their courage, loyalty, and will to survive against an ancient evil that knew no mercy.

In the end, the fate of Stapleford rested on Caroline's shoulders. Through a harrowing struggle, she faced the darkness head-on, discovering the strength she had long buried within herself. The enigmatic newcomer's power waned as the community rallied against him, unearthing the secrets of the town's haunted history.

With the last vestiges of evil banished, Caroline Donald brought closure to her own haunted past and found a semblance of peace in the town she once feared. Stapleford would forever bear the scars of the malevolent force that had once gripped it, but its people emerged stronger, bound together by a shared tale of terror and survival.

And so, the shadows of Stapleford were exorcised, leaving behind a town forever changed, forever haunted, by the memories of its darkest hour. Unrepentant memories, a permanent reminder that good hadn't always won out.

CHAPTER FIVE

The blank page…

COMEUPPANCE
April Berry

Jeff stared into the distance; anything was better than looking down at the grave of his partner. He needed to keep his eyes averted as he could not take a chance on anyone being able to read his true feelings.

His partner was a well-respected member of the community, and her passing was a complete shock to everybody, including Jeff. Finally, the priest offered a final prayer, and the mourners started to disperse; some lingered a few moments longer to pay their final respects.

As darkness fell over the cemetery, a sense of quiet reverence settled in. The only sound was the soft rustling of leaves in the trees and the distant chirping of crickets. The grave of the deceased was marked with a simple headstone, bearing their name and the dates of her birth and death.

The next morning, Jeff woke up and wandered round the large house on the outskirts of the village, looking in every room on his way to the kitchen. What he was looking for he wasn't sure, but when he settled in the kitchen with his coffee, toast, and newspaper, he knew that he would have to start thinking about his future. A future, only last week, he thought would be vastly different.

Jeff and Julie had talked about what they would do when they retired, the places they would visit, and the memories that they would make. Most of the planning had been Julie's doing, whilst Jeff was thinking about Susan, the new addition to his team in the office.

Jeff wondered what would now happen to the business. Would he be able to run things as efficiently as Julie did, continuing to make the strategic decisions that enabled them to live the affluent lifestyle they did?

His mobile ringing pierced his thoughts. Answering it, he could hear the shrill squawk of Tammy on the other end of the phone. Tammy was Julie's daughter from her marriage to Gavin, one which Jeff had successfully blown apart 10 years ago. He had manically pursued Julie until she crumbled under his relentless compliments, romantic dates, and frantic sex whenever the opportunity allowed.

Jeff loved Julie, but Susan, well, she was just a distraction when Julie was working late, away on business, or visiting Tammy, which Julie must do as Tammy would not come anywhere near the house. She hated Jeff, and that hate was now spilling out down the phone to him. He was being blamed for her mother's death, which couldn't be further from the truth, but he would never be able to convince Tammy of that.

The rest of the week for Jeff passed in a blur. He visited the workplace but didn't linger, only to reassure Susan that nothing had changed. He needed to be careful about seeing her for a while until things were sorted.

By that, Jeff meant the sorting of probate and all the other things that needed to be done when someone died – solicitors to see, wills to be read, estate sorted. The first thing Jeff was looking to do when he received the inheritance, and the business was transferred to his sole ownership, was to move. He was bored living in a little village, but the 6-bedroom house Julie owned was a bigger pull than a one-bed flat in the city.

Jeff estimated that he was due to inherit around ten million. He knew the worth of the business, the price of the house, and more or less the value of Julie's pension fund. He also knew that Julie had left it all to him in her will, well except for money to ensure that Tammy was ok.

Jeff and Tammy were due to meet with Julie's solicitors the next day, something that Jeff was not looking forward to. He knew how Tammy would react; more vitriol was coming his way, but in Jeff's mind, tomorrow would be the very last time he would need to ever see her, and boy was he glad.

The next morning, Jeff and Tammy were in the solicitor's foyer, glaring at each other, but even Tammy had the foresight not to make a scene in there.

Eventually, they were called into Mr. Thompson's office and were sat next to each other across the desk from him. Jeff wasn't really concentrating as he should be and missed what Mr. Thompson was saying, not that that mattered, Jeff knew what was in the will because they had both made their wills at the same time 5 years ago in this very office.

"Jeff, are you listening?" said Mr. Thompson, Jeff dragged his attention to the person sat at the other side of the desk, who was talking to him with a not very sympathetic tone.

"So, as I was saying, you have 28 days to vacate the property. Tammy will be taking over the running of the business, and Julie left this letter for you."

Jeff turned white; what was happening? Mr. Thompson handed him an envelope, "Julie left this for you; she came into the office about a month ago. She knew she was dying but didn't want anyone to know."

Slowly, Jeff opened the letter and pulled out an almost blank sheet of paper with only one sentence written on it: "Susan can look after you now."

GHOST WRITER
Carolyn Ward-Daniels

The girls had let themselves in from school and were sitting at the kitchen table with their homework in front of them when their mother arrived home from work. "Good girls," she said as she bustled in and did a quick survey of the kitchen. Milly announced, "Chloe hasn't done any."

Her mother glanced at her eldest. "Get on with it, Chloe. We'll need the table for tea."

"I haven't actually got to do anything right now," Chloe replied. In front of her was a writing pad, the page was blank apart from the date. "We're doing a project about dreams and their meanings; we've got to take the pad to bed and when we wake up, write down any dreams we've had before we forget, and then we're going to analyse them."

"Sounds stupid," said Milly.

"I think it will be great. I'm not good at remembering my dreams."

"You're not great at remembering anything, Chloe. Now come on, you two, out of my way."

Chloe placed the open pad and pen ready on her bedside so she wouldn't forget to do it later; her memory only sparked into action in Maths and science. Both girls went to bed at the same time, being as they shared a bedroom, though Chloe argued that at 14, she ought to be able to stay up later, as when she was Milly's age, 12, she had to go to bed at 8.30. The compromise was 9.30, and 10 pm was strictly lights out.

Their alarms would go off simultaneously at 7.15. Neither sibling was in a hurry to get out of bed. Chloe lazily swung her legs over the side, and then she saw her pad. "Oh... what!... I must have... I can't remember writing anything!"

Milly pulled her duvet away from her mouth. "What are you on about?"

"Something's written on the pad."

"You must have had a dream and written it down in the night."

"I can't remember writing anything!" Chloe picked up the pad. "Oh noooo...oo."

"What's up?" Milly raised up on one elbow, watching her sister go pale and wide-eyed.

"It says, 'I watched you sleeping, snoring, tossing, and turning. Maybe we could chat soon.' Oh my God... something's been in here and written this!... Oh my God, we're being haunted!"

Milly ducked back under the duvet. She could hear Chloe repeating 'Oh my God' and leave the room calling 'Muuuuum,' she raced after her.

"Muuum, I think we've got a ghost!"

"What!"

"Look what was written in the night."

Her mother read it and then glanced at Milly, now sat at the breakfast table. She dropped the pad at Chloe's elbow and said to her youngest, "Milly, you look as white as a ghost."

Chloe glared at her sister. "You wrote it!"

"I did not!"

"You did!"

"Not!"

"I'm warning you, Milly."

Their mother carried on her kitchen chores. She had learned not to bother getting involved in the girls' little spats. "Listen, girls, I have 2 days of earlies starting tomorrow. Christ knows I need the overtime. I shall be leaving really early to catch the 6 o'clock bus, so make sure you leave the kitchen tidy, unplug the toaster and kettle, and don't forget to lock the door."

Milly piped up, "I've got my sleepover at Janine's tomorrow."

"Right, remember to take your sleepover stuff with you to school in the morning. On Friday, Chloe, you'll have to remind yourself to check everything before you leave and to lock the door."

Thursday morning, Milly packed her backpack with sleepover things. They were about to wash the breakfast pots when Milly said, "Oh no, I forgot to ask Mum to write me a note for the games mistress."

"What for?"

"To say I'm on my period and can't have a shower."

"I didn't know you were on your period, and I wouldn't go on a sleepover if I was."

"I'm not, but... I hate having a communal shower, it's embarrassing."

"I know what you mean. Just tell Miss Wagner you're on your period."

"That totally embarrasses me as well. It's all new to me. I go all red and stutter. I hate it. It's much easier just to give her a note."

"Alright, I'll write you a note. You finish the washing up; I'll go do it. I'll filch one of Mum's envelopes."

Chloe handed the sealed envelope to Milly. "Ah, thanks Sis. Don't forget I'm going straight to Janine's after school. It's her birthday, and we're going to the pictures and McDonald's."

"Good; Mum and I can have curry that you don't like."

It took a few seconds after waking up in complete silence for Chloe to remember that she was alone in the house. She sat up to check the time on her phone; she froze. There was a scrawled message on the writing pad. Her scream bounced off the bedroom walls; she snatched up her phone. She had goose pimples all over as she manically swiped at her phone to find her Mum.

"Calm down, Chloe. I told you to only phone me at work in an emergency."

"It is an emergency! I'm scared; a ghost has been again, and it's coming back!"

"What!"

"It left a note... it even signed their name!" Her voice now had the croak of fear and tears. "It says 'I saw you were asleep' 'P. Ekit' 'See you later.' It's not funny, Mum!"

"Chloe, I wrote the note to remind you to take your P.E. Kit."

"But the writing's all scrawly."

"It was a bit dark, you Muppet."

Meanwhile, Milly was awake and thinking she had no regrets about scaring Chloe with that note after she had the major embarrassment of trying to explain the blank piece of paper in the envelope to Miss Wagner.

THE LONELY WRITER
Daizi Rae

Let me introduce you to Sarah Spondergasp, she was a lonely writer. She'd been writing for years, but had never shown her work to anyone. Every time she finished a story, she would read it over and over again, picking it apart, convinced it was terrible. Sarah had always struggled with self-doubt. She was afraid that if she shared her work with anyone else, they would judge her harshly or criticise her writing. So she kept her stories to herself, almost like a secret, and they sat and gathered dust hidden away in a drawer.

One day, while browsing her local second hand book shop, Sarah stumbled upon a book called "The Lonely Writer's Guide to Overcoming Self-Doubt". Intrigued, she picked it up and started flicking through the pages. The book was filled with tips and strategies for writers who struggled with self-doubt, and Sarah found herself nodding along, agreeing with what she was reading on each of the pages.

One of the first things the book suggested was finding a writing group or a critique partner. Sarah had never considered this before, because she thought it was just another reason to be told her writing was rubbish. But, the more she thought about it, the more it had started to make sense. Maybe if she shared her work with other people, she could get some constructive feedback and improve her writing.

So Sarah mustered up the courage to attend a local writing group she'd found online that met near her home. She was nervous at first, but everyone was friendly and supportive. They listened to her story and gave her some feedback, pointing out the parts they liked and offering suggestions for improvement.

At first, Sarah was offended and defensive. She wanted to protect her writing, to defend every word she had written. But then she realised that the feedback was helping her. It was giving her a new perspective on her story, and helping her see areas where she could make it stronger or more engaging.

Encouraged by her experience with the writing group, Sarah started sharing her work more and more. She found a critique partner online and exchanged stories with them, getting even more feedback and suggestions for improvement. With each new round of feedback, Sarah's confidence grew.

But even with all the positive feedback, Sarah still struggled with self-doubt. She would read a story and convince herself it was terrible, even when others had praised it. So she turned to the book for more guidance.

The book suggested writing affirmations, positive statements about herself and her writing that she could repeat to herself whenever she felt doubt creeping in. So Sarah started writing affirmations like "I am a talented writer", "My stories are unique and compelling", and "I am worthy of success."

At first, it felt silly to repeat these affirmations to herself. But over time, they started to sink in. Sarah began to believe in herself and her abilities, and the doubt began to fade away.

Then one day, Sarah decided to submit one of her stories to a literary magazine. She was nervous, but she reminded herself of all the positive feedback she had received and repeated her affirmations. To her surprise, the story was accepted for publication.

It was a small victory, but it meant the world to Sarah. It was proof that her writing was good enough, that she was good enough. And it was all thanks to the guide that had helped her overcome her self-doubt.

From that day forward, Sarah continued to write and share her work. She still struggled with doubt from time to time, but she now had the tools to overcome it. And she knew that with perseverance and a little help from her new found writing community, she could achieve anything she set her mind to.

However, as Sarah's writing career started to take off, she became increasingly obsessed with success. She was no longer content with simply writing for the love of it; now she needed to be recognised, to be the best.

Her writing became less about telling a story and more about impressing others. She became ruthless in her pursuit of success, sacrificing her own happiness and relationships for the sake of her writing career.

Her writing group and critique partner noticed the change in her writing, and tried to gently suggest that she was losing sight of what was important. But Sarah was convinced that this was what she needed to do to make it in the writing world.

Eventually, Sarah's writing became so cold and calculating that it lost all of its heart and soul. Her readers stopped connecting with her stories, and she stopped connecting with herself.

In the end, Sarah was left with a financially successful writing career, but no friends, no family, and no happiness. She had let her obsession with success consume her, and it had cost her everything. But did she care - she did not.

GEOFFREY
George Thomson

Geoffrey's footsteps echoed softly against the empty street as he wandered aimlessly, his troubled thoughts weighing heavy on his heart. The sky above was painted in hues of grey, mirroring the gloom that had settled within him. For most of his life, Geoffrey had felt invisible, a mere silhouette in a world that seemed too busy to notice his presence. His gentle nature and quiet demeanour had often rendered him unheard, his voice drowned out by the cacophony of louder, more assertive individuals.

Geoffrey believed in the power of listening, of lending an ear to those around him so they could feel valued and heard. He cherished the conversations he had with his friends, absorbing their joys and sorrows with unwavering attention. But as the years passed, his friends became accustomed to his quiet companionship, taking his presence for granted. Their conversations became one-sided, their words flowing freely while Geoffrey's contributions faded into the background.

Even his two boys, whom he loved dearly, seemed to have inherited the gift of chatter. They spoke excitedly, sharing their experiences and aspirations, but rarely paused to listen. Geoffrey longed for their understanding, for the simple act of lending an ear to his own worries and fears. But how could he burden them when they had grown accustomed to his silent support?

Geoffrey's health had been deteriorating lately, the weight of his ailments leaving him weakened and vulnerable. Yet, he found himself unable to voice his struggles, fearing they would be met with indifference or brushed aside like a whisper in the wind. The thought of being dismissed, of his pain going unnoticed, made the prospect of discussing his problems even more daunting.

Seeking solace, Geoffrey embarked on a long walk that day, hoping the open air and solitude would grant him clarity. Each step he took seemed to carry him further away from the world he had known, the world where his presence had faded into the shadows. As his footsteps traced a path along the coastline, his thoughts danced with the crashing waves.

As he walked, Geoffrey contemplated writing letters to his family and friends instead of speaking to them directly. Maybe, just maybe, his words would reach their hearts in a way that his voice never could. With trembling hands, he would pour his soul onto paper, exposing his vulnerabilities and hopes, the things he could never utter aloud.

But the further he walked, the heavier his heart became, and the harder it was to find the right words. The pen scratched against the paper, but the ink seemed unable to convey the depth of his emotions. Each sentence fell short, leaving him feeling defeated and unheard once again. He wondered if it was futile, if his words would ever break through the barrier of indifference that surrounded him.

As Geoffrey's footsteps continued to carry him, a single tear escaped his eye, merging with the mist that hung in the air. He yearned for someone to notice his pain, to offer a comforting hand, to listen without judgment. But the fear lingered, gnawing at his resolve, whispering that no one truly cared anymore.

Lost in his despair, a gust of wind tugged at Geoffrey's coat, almost as if it was urging him to stop, to turn back. The world around him seemed to hold its breath, as if waiting for him to find the courage to speak, to share the burden that weighed so heavily upon him.

Geoffrey halted, his gaze fixed on the distant horizon. He realised that even though the road seemed infinite, there were people who cared, people who were waiting to listen, if only he would let them. His silence had inadvertently shielded him from their understanding, from the empathy he so desperately craved.

With renewed determination, Geoffrey turned his steps, retracing the path he had taken. Each stride became a declaration, a vow to reclaim his voice and reach out to those who loved him. The journey ahead might be difficult, but he knew that opening up, expressing his pain and needs, was the only way to bridge the gap that had grown between him and his loved ones.

Geoffrey resolved to cherish his own worth, to make his presence known. He would no longer fade into the background, no longer allow his voice to be muffled by the noise of others. With each word he would write, each conversation he would initiate, Geoffrey would remind the world that he, too, deserved to be seen, heard, and understood. And so, he walked on, a glimmer of hope illuminating his path. The road ahead might still be filled with challenges, but Geoffrey had found the strength to face them head-on. His steps became lighter, his heart filled with a newfound resilience, and his belief in the power of connection was reignited.

CHAPTER SIX

Teamwork. What does that bring to mind for you? Work? Family? Strangers pulling together? The following four stories are what it said to our writers...

OVER THE HILL
Jayne Love

This was my last summer break before going to the big
school; I was 11. I wasn't a very social child. I spent most of my
time on my own, playing in the massive deer park, which was
an extension of our front garden. Feeding the animals on the
farm, playing tennis against the garden wall, rollerskating, or
riding my bike.

Occasionally, I would play hide-n-seek, football, and cricket
with the other kids in the village. And sometimes go fishing or
shooting with the older lads. "Be in by dark" was the basic rule,
but hunger usually got me in way before dark.

One day, I was riding my bike alone on the country lanes. I'd
got off to walk up the hill, pushing my bike. I was thinking, "Is
this why it's called a push bike?" When I got to the top, I got
back on to freewheel down the other side. I heard a car, turned
my head to see it come speeding over the brow of the hill. I
thought it's going to hit me, I tried to scramble out of the way.
Not fast enough, the pain was excruciating as the car struck me.

I woke up with a wall about five feet in front of me. I could
see my leg was bleeding. My shoulder and my arm hurt so
much, and I couldn't move. I called out, but I knew no one was
there. I was getting scared. I tried to move, but I was in so much
pain I passed out again.

When I came around, it was going dark. I prayed it was dusk
and that it wasn't going to rain. I was hungry. I did have a bottle
of juice attached to my crossbar. One of my mom's insistences.
"You need to keep hydrated, take a bottle of pop." I could see it,
but it was just out of reach. I shuffled closer. 'Got it,' my fingers
weren't working. I wedged the bottle between the top of my legs
and, with my left hand, I managed to open the bottle. Even
getting it to my mouth was a struggle. I got a drink, it was the
best ever. I loosely put the top back on and put it to the side of
me. My leg was bleeding again. I was feeling cold and a little
sick too.

I heard something. Was it a voice? There it was again, yes, it
was voices. I shouted then listened, it went quite. Was I
dreaming? I'm sure I heard chatting. I shouted again. "Hello, do

you need assistance? Where are you?" A man's voice spoke with an accent. I said, "Over here, over the wall."

I saw a man and a woman coming over the wall, then another couple appeared at the wall. They came over to me, and the woman said, "Try not to move; you need to keep still. That looks like a compound fracture."

I started to feel warmer; they were covering me with sleeping bags. "What can we do?" the man over the wall said. The older man asked me my name and if I knew where there was a phone. I told him back in the Village about 3 miles away. They spoke together, too quietly for me to hear, then the girls sat down next to me. They told me the men had gone to the village to phone for an ambulance. "Not long now," one said, smiling as she held the bottle to my lips. They spoke to each other, but I must have drifted off to sleep or passed out again. I felt them jump up, and I heard an engine approach. It stopped, and I heard a familiar voice. It was Mickey, the owner of the farm. The two men had flagged him down. He'd driven them to the phone box and back to us. The ambulance arrived. Two men carefully put me onto a board, and the four of them lifted me over the wall into the ambulance and off to the hospital. They gave me something for the pain, and I was unconscious again.

I woke up in the hospital. I had a dislocated left shoulder, a fracture in the right lower arm, a compound fracture of the left lower leg, and a broken ankle. I had a plaster on nearly every limb. The Police came with my mom, and they took a statement. All I could tell them was it was a dark colour Austin 1100. They were never caught.

I had to stay in the hospital for a couple of weeks, off my feet for another 6 weeks, then physio. The hikers, the Ambulance men, and the Hospital staff made a great team, all coming together to help one 11-year-old kid. I wrote and thanked the Hikers, who I found out were Austrians.

I started my new school 6 weeks after the other 1st years, not so good for an already socially awkward kid, but I recovered from my ordeal completely.

TEAMWORK
Sandy Biddles

Ying and Li were born to the same dam and one year apart. However, an uninformed observer would not guess they were siblings. Ying was a chestnut, sturdy in build and temperament, nearly a hand taller than her younger sister, with chubby, rosy cheeks begging to be nuzzled and to nuzzle; Li was more timid, refined, and delicate, with huge velvet eyes dominating her downy face.

Since the bombing had ceased, Shenshin Farm lay starkly abandoned in a no-man's land. The sisters had retreated to the safety and shelter of the nearby 5000-acre forest, whilst most of the other animals had remained or scattered. Some eventually would die from the inability to, or belief that they could not, feed or fend for themselves.

The cataclysm, when it came, had taken everyone by shock and awe. None more so than Farmer Tao and his wife Jing, their farm being remote, and their lives enclosed within its bounds. Together and at length, they studied the mushroom-shaped clouds and the rainbow-hued auroras on all visible horizons.

"The time has come, Jing, my dear. Let us go to the mountains to be close to the spirits," said Tao, trembling inwardly. He saddled and bridled the two strongest cobs. After opening all doors to stables and pens, leaving the inhabitants to their fate, husband and wife set off on their long journey in stoic silence.

Now the young fillies were free of confinement, together but alone in the forest. Ying, the elder, felt an acute sense of exhilaration tempered with responsibility towards her sister. There was abundant food in the forest and streams fed by springs from the mountains in the distance. Their verdant surroundings seemed to welcome and embrace them. But particularly noticeable was the silence and stillness; no birdsong, no rustling of leaves or creaking of branches.

To begin with, Li, in particular, missed the company of others and the regular routine and heartbeat of the farm. As days passed and nights were spent bedded down in the shelter of the thickets, the sisters were joined by three of the hens, the pig Kai, and the old goat Shi. There were plenty of resources to go round, and any old rivalries had been left behind on the farm.

All Spring and Summer, the survivors remained deep in the forest for fear of what might be beyond. Despite their peaceful existence and newfound freedom, a fog of unspoken uncertainty and fear of the unknown clung to their hearts.

As the weather became colder and wetter, and many of the trees lost their leaves, the animals stayed in the thickets and under shelter, creating warmth and comfort from each other and nature's blankets. They would venture out only when necessary until an early Spring morning revealed weak sunlight filtering through the canopy accompanied by a light breeze and the chattering call of a jay, followed by a reply.

Kai grunted in his nest of twigs and straw. Shi opened her eyes, pricked her ears, and listened. Ying raised her head from Li's warm withers, stretched her hind legs, and stood up, careful not to trample the hens who were already running around in confusion.

A team meeting over breakfast ensued to decide what to do.

"We're happy enough in the forest and have all we need," cried the eldest hen. "Why risk our necks in the outside world?"

"But we may have the chance to better ourselves...have our own home...help others to follow our example," intervened Kai. "I have heard that the world is full of opportunities for all."

"If the world has ended, that is foolish and impossible," bleated Shi.

After much debate, the band, in order of size, tallest first, linked up by tails and traveled to the edge of the forest, the jays flitting along behind them; flashes of pink, then blue, from tree to tree, calling each other with excitement.

"Have courage, comrades," called Ying, in the lead, feeling the weight of expectancy and uncertainty behind her broad shoulders.

As they reached the last line of trees, Li gently released Ying's tail and moved to stand alongside her. Flicking their manes to shield their eyes against the brightness, the stark reality of the new world made their resolve waver.

"One day, friends. We are not yet ready," whinnied the ever practical matriarch.

Separately and, for most, with relief, the animals returned to the forest and went about their daily duties; gathering, foraging, tidying before regrouping for dinner and debriefing the morning's events. And so their lives continued to unfold.

As time went on, other animals migrated to the forest from woods and thickets in the province. Zones and encampments became established, each with its own rules and ways of being, some more democratic than others. With good husbandry, it expanded and flourished to supply their needs.

Meanwhile, high on the plateau in the mountains, only visible to the piercing eyes of golden eagles and scavenging vultures, lay messages of human hope written in stones.

THE TEAM PLAYER
Daizi Rae

Gary was an all-round good guy, happily married to Johnathan, father to two sassy-pants daughters, Nicole and Amanda, and one lazy little fur baby, Ruby. Also, if you looked up "team player" in the dictionary, you'd probably find a photo of Gary. You couldn't hope to find a more people-oriented person if you searched for the rest of your days. He prided himself on his ability to work well with others, to collaborate, and to compromise. So, when he joined the MAD [Making A Difference] team at work, he was eager to get to work with his colleagues to improve the work lives of everyone across the business.

Robert was the first person on the team to welcome him, and Gary was grateful for his kindness. They quickly bonded over their shared interests in cycling and art, and Gary was thrilled to have made a new friend at work. As the weeks went on, Gary found himself relying as much on Robert's expertise and experience as Robert did on his. They made a great team, bouncing ideas off of one another.

But then, something changed. Gary started noticing that Robert was taking credit for his ideas. He assumed, at first, that it was just a slip of the tongue and Robert meant to say "we" instead of "I." But by the second and third time it happened, Gary was sure that Robert was just using him as an ideas man. That, and the fact that Robert had started belittling him in front of the rest of the team, hurt Gary deeply. He felt betrayed and used. He tried to confront Robert about it, but Robert brushed him off and told him to stop being so sensitive.

The tension between them continued to grow. Gary stopped sharing ideas with Robert and instead took them straight to their manager himself. That stopped Robert from stealing his ideas, but it didn't stop Robert from belittling him in front of the rest of the team. The situation escalated from there, and Gary became no longer of any use to Robert.

Gary no longer woke up on workdays looking forward to being part of a team. He woke up with a pit of dread in his stomach, and if he could find an excuse to call in sick, he would use it, afraid of what he was walking into at work. Johnathan was worried about his husband and tried to talk it out with him. He suggested that Gary make an appointment with his manager or even HR to address Robert's outrageous behaviour. The problem, as Gary saw it by this point, was that he would look even weaker by complaining than he already looked, constantly being publicly undermined. So, he didn't say anything, and every day was a little bit worse than the day before. Gary stopped smiling, stopped taking care of himself, stopped believing in himself, and his mood went from disappointed, to hurt, to humiliated, and eventually to angry. And that's when things took a decidedly bleak turn.

Gary could take it no longer. Enough was enough. One day, after a particularly heated argument where Robert was berating Gary for being the weak, pathetic individual he saw him to be while walking up the stairs from the canteen to their office, where no one was there to witness his behaviour, Gary snapped. In a fit of blind rage, he grabbed the back of Robert's head and with all his frustration and rage, he smashed Robert's face onto the stair rail with all his might, killing him instantly.

Gary was immediately consumed with guilt and regret. He stared at Robert and couldn't believe what he had done. He knew that this would ruin his life and his entire family. Not to mention the lives of Robert's loved ones. He should turn himself in to the authorities immediately.

Images of being sat in a cell, awaiting trial, being sentenced to life for murder, plagued Gary's mind. He couldn't help but wonder how things had gone so wrong. His own insecurities had gotten the best of him. He had let his anger cloud his judgment, and now, he would pay the price.

Gary walked into the men's restroom just off the stairwell and stood looking at himself in the mirror. He looked so ordinary. He wasn't a murderer at heart, was he?

When he heard the first screams from the stairwell as Robert was discovered by their colleagues, Gary walked out of the restroom and was as shocked as everyone else. "OMG, what a tragic accident!"

NOT TONIGHT
George Thomson

In the heart of Sherwood Forest, nestled amongst the lush greenery, stood a secluded cabin where Petra and Steve had retreated for a weekend away. They had a tradition of playing an adult husband and wife game, one that required trust, communication, and an understanding of each other's boundaries. It was a game that strengthened their connection and deepened their love. But this time, Petra was not in the mood to play.

As Steve set the stage, dimming the lights and adorning the bedstead with handcuffs and silk scarves, Petra's heart sank. She had been feeling off since they arrived, and the thought of indulging in their usual game seemed exhausting. However, she didn't want to disappoint her husband, so she tried to put on a brave face.

"Lie down, my love," Steve said, his voice thick with excitement. "Trust me, as always. If you ever want to stop, just use our safe word."

Petra hesitated for a moment but eventually complied, lying on the bedspread with her arms and legs spread-eagled, awaiting the touch of the silk scarves. But as Steve loomed over her, she felt an unexpected wave of anger and humiliation wash over her. She realised she had never properly communicated her feelings about the game and how it sometimes made her uncomfortable.

Steve leaned in closer, his eyes gleaming with desire. "Are you ready, darling?"

Feeling vulnerable and uncertain, she managed a weak nod. "Yes, but can we take it slow tonight?"

"Of course," Steve assured her, not realising the turmoil inside Petra's mind.

He began to bind her wrists gently, but as he leaned over to get another scarf, Petra felt a surge of panic. She had to speak up before her discomfort escalated further.

"Steve, I don't think I want to do this tonight," she said, her voice quivering with emotion.

Steve stopped, looking confused. "Are you sure, Petra? We can stop if you're not feeling up to it."

Tears welled up in Petra's eyes as she mustered the strength to be honest with her husband. "I don't want to play the game tonight, or maybe ever again. It's just not something I enjoy."

Steve's face fell, and he released her from the handcuffs immediately. "I'm so sorry, Petra. I didn't know you felt this way. We should have talked about it before."

Guilt gnawed at Petra's heart as she realised she should have been more open about her feelings. But it was too late now, and she needed time to process her emotions. She excused herself, needing to be alone for a while, and retreated to the bedroom's small balcony, where she could feel the cool forest breeze on her face.

Steve gave her space, pondering how he had failed to notice her true feelings. In the cabin's silence, he heard her sobs echoing through the rooms, and his heart ached with regret.

As Petra stood alone, her mind spiralled into fear and anxiety. Her imagination ran wild with thoughts of being left helpless in the cabin while Steve ventured out for help, only to meet a terrible fate. A shiver ran down her spine as she realised how isolated and vulnerable they were in the middle of Sherwood Forest.

Meanwhile, Steve decided to go for a walk, hoping the fresh air might clear his mind and provide clarity. He didn't want to leave Petra alone, but he also didn't want to pressure her into talking before she was ready.

Back in the cabin, Petra's fear intensified. The voices in her head chattered, blending with the sounds of the forest. The floorboard creaked, making her heart race as she imagined someone watching her from the shadows.

Outside, Steve's thoughts were consumed with Petra's wellbeing. As he walked deeper into the forest, he realised that he had made a grave mistake by not prioritising their open communication about their desires and boundaries. He vowed to change, to be more attentive and understanding of Petra's feelings.

Suddenly, the peaceful ambiance of the forest was interrupted by a cry for help. Steve's heart pounded as he recognised his wife's voice. He sprinted back to the cabin, praying that she was safe.

Inside, Petra's distress had reached its peak. She had accidentally knocked over a lamp in her distress, causing a small fire to ignite. The flames spread rapidly, and she found herself trapped and unable to escape.

Steve rushed into the cabin, his heart sinking at the sight of the fire. He acted quickly, grabbing a nearby blanket to smother the flames and rescue his love.

"I'm so sorry, Petra," he said, tears streaming down his face. "I should have listened to you and understood how you were feeling."

As the fire subsided, Petra looked into her husband's eyes, realising the true depth of his remorse and love for her. "I should have been more open with you, too," she admitted. "We both made mistakes."

They held each other tightly, their bodies shaking with fear and relief. It was a turning point in their relationship, one that would lead them to rebuild their trust and redefine the boundaries of their intimacy.

In the following days, Petra and Steve talked openly and honestly, learning to respect each other's feelings and desires. They discovered new ways to connect and found that true intimacy came from mutual understanding and unwavering support.

As they left Sherwood Forest, hand in hand, they knew that their love had grown stronger through the trials they had faced together. Their game might have taken a dark turn, but it had ultimately brought them closer, reminding them that true teamwork and safe words were not just aspects of their game but essential elements of their marriage.

Petra gripped Steves hand tighter, smiling across at him while silently plotting his demise.

CHAPTER SEVEN

The stories in this chapter had no writing prompt. So the following stories are personally inspired by each writer individually. Let's see where their minds wander when left unchecked...

I"LL NEVER FORGET MY FIRST LOVE
(It was meant to last forever)
Ceejhay Walker

Keith's POV:

I hummed "Queen of My Heart" by Westlife as I walked under the rain with my umbrella. Looking ahead, I saw a feminine figure seated on the sidewalk, completely drenched. I glanced around and saw that there were no places she could stay to hide herself from the rain. Should I help... or should I not? I questioned myself as I got even closer to where she was. With a sigh, I walked up to her and put the umbrella over her head. She noticed as she looked up. Our eyes met, and time seemed to stop. She had the most beautiful eyes... Wait, what? I blinked several times and looked away as I paused my music and cleared my throat.

"I'm headed towards the state's library. If you want, we could share my umbrella," I said as I scratched my hair with my free hand.

Her lips curled in a smile, and I felt my heart skip a beat. "Thank you. I'm headed to the library as well," she said as she stood up. I smiled back and positioned the umbrella in a way that we could both share it.

"I'm Amy," she said as we walked down the walkway.

"My name's Keith," I replied.

The pitter-patter of the raindrops hitting the soil below me slowly brought me back to the present. The merciless raindrops hit my head, shoulder, and wherever else they could touch as I suddenly remembered where I was. It had been a year since we first met, but it felt like it was only yesterday. All of the memories we shared came flooding back to me as I stood there. The times we had spent underneath the stars, the first time we kissed, the day I proposed—the memories were endless.

A ghost of a smile graced my lips as I still remembered the way her smile lit up the room, the sound of her laughter, and the warmth of her touch. "Do you remember the day we met, Amy? It was raining just like this," I said with a smile as I looked up. "Still funny how I never told you that you were my first love," I let out a sad laugh. "I thought I had seen the most beautiful creature ever," I chuckled. "Well, I wasn't wrong," I whispered, my voice breaking.

As I stood under the same rain that brought us together, my eyes met her gravestone. The memory of the day she suddenly left me without warning flashed through my mind. I shook my head and dropped the bouquet of dandelions I had brought on her grave. I took several steps back, my gaze never leaving her gravestone until my heart began to ache. I shut my eyelids as I felt tears freely escape my eyes and mix with the rain that fell on my face. My shoulders heaved as a sob escaped my lips, a sob I had held in for far too long.

A cold breeze blew, and I suddenly felt like I was wrapped in warm arms. It felt like the warm and loving hugs you used to... My eyelids flew open, and the sobs immediately stopped. I froze when I saw no one in front of me and felt cold again. It couldn't be... could it? My eyes met her gravestone once more. After a few minutes of staring, my lips curled up in a smile. It was you. My smile widened. I took a deep breath as I turned and walked away from her grave. "I understand. I'll never forget you, my love," I whispered to myself.

Amy's POV:

Tears slowly slipped from my eyes as I watched my first love break down in front of my new home. "Keith..." I called out, but I knew, I knew he couldn't hear me. He's in a different world, Amy—a world where you're gone, I reminded myself.

"Do you remember the day we met, Amy? It was raining just like this," I heard him say.

"Of course, I remember. How could I ever forget?" I responded with a smile.

"Still funny how I never told you that you were my first love," he laughed as he said this.

"You were mine too," I responded with a shaky laugh.

"I thought I had seen the most beautiful creature ever," he chuckled. "Well, I wasn't wrong," he said, his voice breaking. I watched with a smile as he dropped the bouquet of dandelions he held by my grave and burst into a heart-wrenching sob. Tears filled my eyes as I made my way to him. "Keith..." I stood in front of him and reached out to dry his tears, but my hands passed through him. "Please, please, stop crying. I'm fine; I'm really fine," I cried out. I opened my arms wide and made an attempt to embrace him.

My eyes widened when I felt the warmth of his skin and his heart beat as my head rested on his chest. However, it only lasted for a split second, as I fell through him just as quickly as I had touched him. "What just happened?" I asked myself as I got up from the ground. I turned and saw him staring at my gravestone once again with a smile. "Well, you're not crying anymore," I smiled.

He turned away, and I heard him whisper the words, "I understand. I'll never forget you, my love."

"I'll never forget you either, my love," I spoke quietly to his retreating back. A bright light suddenly appeared at my side, and I felt its pull, telling me that it was time. I turned back to Keith, who was already at a distance. "At least, I know he'll be fine now." With a smile, I walked towards the light.

THE LONG FURLOUGH
Carolyn Ward-Daniels

I've come to dislike Monday breakfast more so now than when I was in work. There is a fractious atmosphere that doesn't dissolve with the clinking of breakfast activity. I can sense the weight of disapproval tumbling out of Jane as she levels her glances at my pyjamas, still on me as I eat my toast. She's just nodded toward the pile of ironing, saying, "I'm glad it was fine this weekend and I managed to get all that washing done and dried," which is code for "you could have cut the lawn while it was fine and get the ironing done, Dave."

"Do you want another cup of tea?" I ask her, knowing she's on the verge of running late so won't want one, but it seems like I'm looking after her.

"No, got to go, could be late again tonight. We are still short-staffed."

"Text me when you're leaving then, I can get the oven on."

"Dave, I have prepped and filled the slow cooker. Just remember to switch it on at 11. I'm sick of oven chips and chicken."

I pick up some dirty plates; she picks up her phone. "Bye, love," I say. She leaves; she has stopped giving me a kiss goodbye. When she goes, I plonk the crockery down again. I've got all day to sort that out. I'll have another cuppa while I read yesterday's paper.

After an hour of failing the crossword and reading doom and gloom, I decide to get dressed, but the bed looks enticing. I'll just have twenty minutes. The twenty minutes slips into an hour, and I still have to force myself upright. My phone is telling me I have a text.

"Turn on the slow cooker!"

Honestly, has she installed a camera? It looks really dull outside now. I pull my jogging bottoms on, my regular daily suit recently. Every day's a Sunday. I thought I would be having a three-month paid holiday, but because Jane is having to work, she expects me to do the household chores, like that tower of ironing. Maybe if I bandaged my wrist and said I fell over and sprained it... No, she'd know, being a nurse. I got away with the pretend Covid, isolating in bed for a week.

Looking through the patio windows, the weather was really turning. The wind was punching the fences and bending the trees. The empty watering can did an ungainly meander across the garden. I did a swift risk assessment and thought it made sense to put it away out of the wind and away from the French windows. Just made it back in as splinters of rain tapped at the window and fast grew into a heavy downpour. Well, at least I won't have to mow the lawn. Mind you, I'd rather do that than the ironing. I'm beginning to not miss work, and I can sneak a cheeky vodka whenever I want. I do keep the downstairs loo spotless so Jane doesn't have to clean it, which means I can hide a bottle behind the bleach in the back of the vanity unit. Actually, I'll have a little vodka and coke now and find something else to read. I'll do the ironing later or tomorrow. There's a glossy magazine that comes with the Sunday paper. I'll have a butchers at that. Oh lovely, perfume, fashion, handbags, more fashion, an article about the menopause, horoscope. I'll read it.

"The lunar eclipse warns that what happens this week may shock you, but the signs are beginning to show through the cracks. This is a timely reminder to not be deflected from your chosen path."

"Who believes this crap? More adverts, more clothes, cordless cleaners, ho ho agony aunt. Let's have a butchers at this for a laugh."

Dear Sally,

I have been married to the same man for twenty-two years. We have 2 kids at university.

"Know all about that love, cheers!"

I work for the NHS, so with the pandemic, I am at work a lot of punishing hours. My husband, however, has been furloughed, and whilst he seems happy about it, I worry that it is affecting him. He has become very idle and a secret drinker. I've found bottles of booze hidden around the house.

"Aye lad, after me own heart, cheers!"

I can smell alcohol on his breath as soon as I get home. He shies away from chores even though he has all the time in the world. I don't know if I can stay in this marriage any longer. I thought I was married to an honest, hardworking man. He even pretended to have Covid so he could stay in bed, and I had to run around after him after a full shift of nursing at work. Do I ask for a divorce?

Unhappy J.

"Oh bugger."

GHOST HUNTER
Daizi Rae

Jamie had been a ghost hunter for almost two decades. During that time, they had helped countless spirits find peace and release them from their earthly binds. Every case was different, and Jamie's methods varied depending on the circumstances. Some ghosts needed to resolve unfinished business, while others simply needed someone to listen to their story. Jamie had always been fascinated by the stories behind the ghosts, and it was this curiosity that kept them going.

As the years passed, Jamie found themselves becoming more introspective. They wondered if their own past had shaped who they were today. Maybe they had forgotten memories that were influencing their behaviour, just like the ghosts they had helped. So, Jamie started to delve into their family history to see if they could uncover anything about their ancestors.

It wasn't long before Jamie stumbled upon an intriguing piece of information. One of their ancestors had worked on a space station in the year 1900. It was a tour of duty, and the ancestor had left behind a wife and twin girls at home, longing for her return. Her name was Eloise.

Jamie couldn't help but wonder what had happened to Eloise. Had she made it back to Earth? Or had something gone wrong? They decided to do some more research to find out.

Jamie spent hours poring over old family records and newspaper clippings, searching for any information on Eloise. They discovered that she had been a pioneering astronaut, one of the first women to venture into space. She had been highly respected in her field and had made significant contributions to space research.

But then, Jamie came across an article that stopped them in their tracks. It was a news report from the year 1900, reporting that the space station Eloise had been on had drifted into a black hole. There were no survivors.

Jamie felt a deep sense of sadness and loss for Eloise, a woman they had never met but who was a part of their family history. They couldn't imagine what it must have been like for

Eloise's family, waiting for her return, only to hear that she had been lost in space.

But as Jamie continued to reflect on Eloise's story, they realised something else. Eloise had been a trailblazer, someone who had dared to explore the unknown and push the boundaries of what was possible. In many ways, Jamie saw themselves in her. They had spent so long chasing ghosts and exploring the mysteries of the past that they had forgotten to live in the present.

Jamie realised that it was time to stop living in the shadows of the past and start creating their own future. They knew that it wouldn't be easy, but they were determined to try. After all, if Eloise could venture into the depths of space, then Jamie could certainly take a few risks in their own life.

Over the next few months, Jamie took small steps to break free from their comfort zone. They tried new hobbies, met new people, and explored different parts of the city. It wasn't always easy, and there were moments when they felt like giving up. But Jamie knew that they had to keep going, just like Eloise had.

And as Jamie looked back on their journey, they realised that they had come a long way. They had let go of their obsession with the past and had started to embrace the present. They had learned that life was full of surprises and that sometimes, the best way to find happiness was to take a chance and explore the unknown.

Jamie still thought about Eloise from time to time, wondering what might have been if she had made it back to Earth. But they no longer felt adrift, like the space station that had taken Eloise away from her family. Instead, Jamie felt anchored, rooted in the present, and excited about the possibilities that lay ahead. That was, until Eloise started visiting!

NO OTHER OPTION
Dean Wrigley

The tumour in Emma's head had almost consumed her. She is in a hospital bed blind, deaf and mute. She only has her senses of taste, smell and touch to tell her what's happening around her.

But her mind is still sharp. She understands her predicament. Teetering on the edge of life. Waiting to die.

She can recognise when her parents, her siblings and friends are there. She can sense their presence. Sometimes she can smell who they are.

She cannot help but feel the tears on their cheeks as they bend to kiss her. Be strong. Tears will change nothing.

Oh! Someone touched her arm! Who was that? Someone new? Emma opened the palm of her hand and began to draw the letters of her name on it. She lifted her hand towards the unknown person hoping they would understand the instruction. The person took her hand and began to move a finger across it spelling out the letters of their name. The first letter 'K'. The second letter 'E'. Emma's anticipation rose and she felt a thrill of excitement. Was it the person she hoped it would be? The third letter 'R'. No, that wasn't the letter she was expecting and her heart sank just a little despite the kindness of this new person coming to visit her. Another letter, another 'R'! Ooh! Perhaps she had been dismissive too soon. A fifth letter 'Y' and she melted into tears, thankfulness and a little annoyance at the formality of the friend she had known since childhood as Kez.

Emma held her friend's hand in both of hers and pressed her face on it. Kerry could feel the dampness of tears on her fingers but didn't pull her hand away. Her own tears streamed down her cheeks and spilled onto the hospital bed and then onto her friend's hands too. Their tears mixed together like brine, salted with their mutual grief at Emma's predicament. Emma looked up towards Kerry, her blind eyes wide, distant, unfocused. She screwed up her face and pouted her lips. Kerry smiled at a memory from long, long ago before moving her own scrunched up face towards Emma's and allowing their lips to touch - something they hadn't done since they were young teenagers, playing dares, investigating their sexuality. As teenagers they had both recoiled in horror and laughter, but here, now, it was a kiss of defeat. A final kiss. A kiss of goodbye.

As their heads parted Kerry took Emma's hand and wrote S O R R Y D R E S S. Emma knew exactly what she was referring to, smiled and patted her old friend's hand.

It had been a Sunday late in summer. Emma and her siblings were on their way home from church while Kerry and her brothers were collecting wild berries. No one could say how it started but a berry war broke out between the families. As berries flew through the air Emma realised she wasn't dressed for the occasion and made a dash for home hoping to be too fast for any soft missile to reach her. But it was a forlorn hope as she felt the splat of a berry on her back, staining her favourite dress forever. Unfortunately, it was Kerry's berry that left its mark. Kerry was devastated about ruining her best friend's favourite dress.

In a flash Emma twisted her torso and stretched out towards the bedside cabinet on the other side of the bed from where Kerry was. Her fingers touched what she expected to be there. She took hold of it and placed it on the bed near Kerry. She assumed her friend would be watching so she tapped the book and held out her hand, repeatedly curling her fingers in a grabbing motion. She felt Kerry's hand in hers. She took hold of it firmly, opened the fingers and began to write on the palm using her own forefinger.

Her first letter was J. Her second was O. Her third letter was B. A pause. Next she wrote 6 followed by 2 1 3. She tapped on the book again and looked up towards her friend hoping she would understand.

Kerry picked up the book and turned it over to see the front cover. The Holy Bible. Kerry understood. She quickly thumbed through the pages to the Book of Job. She found chapter 6. She looked down at Emma.

Emma was unable to hear the words being read to her. She was unable to see the lips that spoke them. All she had was the memory of the words. She imagined her friend reading them and began to paraphrase the essence of their meaning in her own mind.

"The arrows of the Almighty find their mark in me and their poison soaks into my spirit. God's onslaughts wear me away. Why does He taunt me so?
I have no other option than to wait.
I have no other option than to be patient.
I have no other option than to bear this mantle until He hears my request and grants me what I hope for - to be released from this unsparing anguish.
Do I have the strength to wait? I have no other option.
With all the doctors and nurses keeping me alive; I have no other option.
The power to help myself is put out of my reach."

Kerry finished the reading and looked at her pitiful friend seemingly deep in thought. She squeezed Emma's hand. Emma smiled, mouthed the words "Thank you" and settled down on her pillow, still holding Kerry's hand. Eventually her grip relented and their hands separated. Kerry sat at the bedside reading passages from The Holy Bible for another hour as Emma drifted off to sleep.

Emma's family arrived to take up the vigil. They hugged and thanked Kerry for spending some time with her.

During the night the Almighty heard Emma's request and released her from her anguish.

CHAPTER EIGHT

A Bare Book anthology just wouldn't be complete without a chapter of Christmas stories, it's becoming a tradition, and that's how we like it...

THE DAY CHRISTMAS WAS CANCELLED
Daizi Rae

Dan and Hayley woke up on Christmas morning, wondering why it was so quiet. "Where are the kids?" Dan said, looking at the bedside clock. "I thought they'd have woken us up ages ago." They gave each other a puzzled look, slipped out of bed, and put on their slippers before padding through to the kids' room, only to find their beds empty and their Christmas stockings still stuffed with untouched toys. The bedroom window was open, the cookies they left out for Santa had been eaten, and next to the carrots that were left out for Rudolf and the rest of the reindeer was a note.

"Sorry, folks, I'm in the middle of a recession. Had to borrow your kids, my elves have gone on strike. I'll get them back to you right after our last stop in Samoa. See you after lunch, love, Santa."

"Ooooh," said Hayley, "What's the going rate for elves nowadays? Could be a nice little earner."

That earned her such a look from Dan. "I don't care if it's a million pounds or four pennies and a peanut, you don't 'borrow' people's children in the middle of the night like some bleeding kidnapper! What's wrong with you?"

"But it's Santa!" exclaimed Hayley.

"Right," said Dan, "so it's okay to take some random person's kids in the dead of night, as long as they fit an elf costume and are old enough to be potty trained. God forbid Santa has to stop every hour to change nappies."

Hayley burst out laughing. "I'm sorry babe, just got this mental image of Santa delivering dirty nappies instead of presents. Can you imagine the looks on the kids' faces?"

Dan was not amused and stomped downstairs, wondering if he should phone the police and report a kidnapping. But he could just picture their faces, trying hard not to laugh at him while he tried and failed to explain that Santa had kidnapped his children. Merry bloody Christmas!

***

Meanwhile, somewhere over Canada, Santa was grinding his teeth and regretting his rash actions more with every second. He had even gone so far as to wonder if it would cause much hassle if he just dropped these three kids over the side of the sleigh and carried on without them. It's not like he had to be on anyone's naughty or nice list!

Amelia was climbing on Santa's lap while he was trying to navigate Canada's rooftops, tugging at his beard, crying, "This is not a real beard, I saw a robin peeking out of it. Where are you, Mr. Robin?"

Jessica was in floods of tears, sobbing, "I want to go home, I don't like heights. I want my mummy, take me home." All the time trying to climb inside Santa's jacket so she couldn't see how high they were.

Imogen, though, was having the time of her life! She was sitting on top of the sack of presents, pulling them out one by one and throwing them over the side of the sleigh, howling at the top of her voice with every gift, over and over, "Here's another one, Merry Christmas!"

Poor Santa was in despair. He couldn't guide the sleigh in a straight line; he'd missed two whole towns full of kids already, and who knew when he'd be back on track. Not him, that's for sure. He did consider trying to land on the roof of some childless couple and leaving them these three terrors as a gift. But then remembered he was meant to love everyone and he was responsible for these little hooligans. So he tried to find another solution that didn't involve giving the little terrors away; he had promised to deliver them back home for lunchtime after all.

Ah, that's it, he'd take them home now. Better to be late delivering presents on his own - well, the ones that Imogen hadn't thrown over the side yet - than endure this bedlam any longer than necessary. So the reindeer turned the sleigh around and made their way back to Belper in the UK as fast as their little legs and some Christmas magic could muster.

***

Dan and Hayley were sitting in the lounge in front of the fireplace, waiting for Santa to bring back their kids, even though it was only eleven o'clock and lunchtime was still two hours away. When they weren't hugging each other and panicking in case the kids didn't arrive back, they were blaming each other for not locking the window or for not hearing anything while their kids were being kidnapped. How did they sleep through that? It didn't occur to them that no one hears Santa delivering gifts; it's all part of that Christmas magic.

Then they did hear a noise, an almighty thud on their roof, followed by sleigh bells and three very familiar voices complaining bitterly. Loudest of all was Imogen, who did not want to come home; she was having far too much of a good time on the sleigh.

Santa's heavy footsteps could be heard walking toward their chimney, where he dropped Amelia down first, followed by a very grateful Jessica, glad to be home at last. As Dan and Hayley were hugging Amelia and Jessica, waiting for Imogen to drop down the chimney, they could hear a commotion up on the roof. Imogen was clinging onto Santa's jacket, her little hands not letting go of the tops of Santa's pockets. In the struggle, her hand brushed against something in Santa's pocket, so she grabbed it to see what it was. And not a lot of you know this, but Santa has a magic lighter he uses to relight the fires after he has delivered your presents.

Imogen let go of Santa and ran back to the bag of presents on the sleigh, lighter in hand. She wanted to hide and stay with Santa when he left, but Santa was too wily for that and scooped her up to drop her down the chimney, but not before Imogen managed to use the lighter and set fire to the presents for the whole of the rest of the world along with the sleigh, leaving the reindeer to take off into the skies with the charred remains, and leaving Santa stranded on a rooftop in Belper.

And that, dear reader, is how Christmas was canceled.

THE TALE OF WILLIAM PINTER
Dean Wrigley

The light from the full moon pierced through the living room curtains, lighting up the Christmas tree positioned in front of the big window. It was the early hours of the morning, and William Pinter was hiding behind the settee, waiting for Santa's sleigh to arrive. He wanted to catch the red-attired man in the act, just to prove to all his doubting-Thomas school friends that Santa Claus was real.

"How can you still believe in Santa, you idiot? You're 13; you should have been told he's not real by now. Do your parents want you to be a child forever?" his friends had goaded him.

But William was steadfast in his belief. He knew. He just knew Santa was real, and he would provide the proof this Christmas Eve night.

The living room was dark, and it seemed even darker from William's hiding place. The room was almost silent too. The only sound was the gentle ticking of the clock on the mantelpiece and the occasional creak from his parents' bedroom above his head.

William peeked over the top of the settee, looking towards the window. The light from the full moon was scattered by the curtain and sparkled through the Christmas tree fairy lights. Gradually, he became aware that the light coming through the curtains was getting brighter. "This might be the headlights of Santa's sleigh," he whispered to himself. He switched 'record' on his mobile phone and disappeared behind the settee, holding the mobile phone above his head using a selfie stick.

In no time at all, the whole wall and the ceiling over his head were lit up. The last thing William remembered was a series of almighty skids, crashes, and screams. The rest of the story was pieced together by the police from William's mobile phone footage.

The front window wall was completely demolished as a big red Post Office van came careening through it and into the living room. The tree was destroyed; baubles and pine cones were thrown haphazardly around the room. The angel at the top of the tree took flight and was never seen again. The ceiling was sheared through. Numerous joists split, causing William's parents' bed to fall through the hole, landing abruptly half on top of the van before losing balance, toppling over, and tipping its occupants out onto the floor, accompanied with Mrs. Pinter's screams. The van crunched into the settee, pushing it up against the wall, trapping William behind it.

The selfie stick supporting William's mobile phone was pinned against the wall and captured the scene as the dust settled. A man dressed in red with a big white, dusty beard was the first figure that appeared from the haze. 'Santa' ran his fingers through his hair and shook his head. A blizzard of plaster tumbled from his hair and beard. Finally, the man in red spoke.

"What the bloody hell's happened here?" The voice wasn't that of Santa, but of a very confused Mr. Pinter.
A hand reached up and tugged at Mr. Pinter's pyjama bottoms. "Trevor! Trevor! Where are we?" said his wife.

"It looks like we're in our front room. What's left of it more like," said Mr. Pinter.

He bent down and helped his wife get to her feet. "Is that a Post Office van in our front room?" she asked.

"Ee bah gum, so it is," said an astonished Mr. Pinter.

"Is our William OK?" she said.

"He's probably still asleep," said Mr. Pinter, "he could sleep through a bomb dropping."

Together they carefully shuffled through the rubble towards the van. As they got nearer, there was something strange about the passengers. It looked like they were reindeer.

Suddenly, the van door opened, and the reindeer clambered out - each standing on two legs. The mouths of the two humans opened in awe as both reindeer hurriedly found an escape route and ran off into the night.

The humans stood aghast as wailing sirens eventually brought the constabulary into their destroyed front room.

His parents were very surprised when William was found behind the settee. As a precaution, he was taken to the hospital with his parents, but all three were released at breakfast time.

William's mobile phone footage was used in an attempt to identify the reindeer, but no clues were found.

However, William had the evidence he needed. There on his mobile was proof of Santa, dressed in red with a big white beard, accompanied by one of his helpers dressed in green. Also, there were two reindeer who, of course, were never seen again because they must have made their own way back to the North Pole.

At school in the new year, William proudly showed stills captured from his phone footage to his skeptical school friends.

The friends laughed with William as he retold the events of that Christmas Eve. They had seen the aftermath on the local news bulletin, but they let William have his day.

"You may have seen your Santa, but you're still an idiot, William Pinter!" they said.

CHRISTMAS REDEMPTION
George Thomson

The snow fell gently over the small town of Bakersfield, blanketing the streets and rooftops with a pristine layer of white. Christmas lights adorned the houses, casting a warm glow on the otherwise cold winter night. Among the cheerful residents, there was one woman who carried a heavy burden that threatened to extinguish the festive spirit within her.

Brenda Winters, a skilled assassin known for her precise marksmanship, had a reputation that sent shivers down the spines of even the most hardened criminals. Her lethal skills had earned her a place among the world's deadliest killers, but beneath the icy exterior was a heart that longed for redemption. Brenda's conscience had grown heavy with guilt over the years. She couldn't erase the faces of those she had eliminated, even if they were truly bad people. The weight of her sins had become unbearable, and she yearned for a way out of the dark path she had chosen.

As Brenda contemplated retirement, a mysterious message appeared on her encrypted communication channel. The offer was unlike any she had ever seen before – a contract worth an exorbitant amount, promising enough wealth to disappear forever. It seemed like the perfect way out, a chance to leave her dangerous life behind and start anew. Yet, something gnawed at Brenda's instincts. A nagging feeling that this job was different, that there was more at stake than money alone.

Reluctantly, she accepted the contract, hoping that this final job would bring her enough resources to retire and find redemption for her past deeds. As the days passed and Christmas drew nearer, Brenda began preparing for the hit. Her mind was conflicted, torn between her need for redemption and her instincts as a survivor. But she couldn't back down now; the stakes were too high.

Meanwhile, in a quaint little cafe on the outskirts of Bakersfield, Brenda encountered a woman named Lily. There was something unusual about her, an air of mystery that piqued Brenda's interest. As fate would have it, Lily was more than she appeared to be. She had a unique gift – an ability to read people's emotions and intentions, which she used to help others find the right path in life.

On a cold, snowy evening, Lily approached Brenda, sensing the turmoil within her. With compassion in her eyes, Lily said, "I see the weight you carry, Brenda. The path you're on will only lead to darkness. You have a choice to make, and it will define who you truly are."

Brenda was taken aback, her heart racing as she tried to grasp the significance of Lily's words. How could this stranger know so much about her? Brenda was torn between sharing her secrets and maintaining her distance from anyone who could be a potential threat.

"I can help you find the right path," Lily continued, as if she could read Brenda's thoughts. "The path of redemption, of goodness, is still open to you. But you must be willing to change."

As Brenda listened to Lily's words, she felt a glimmer of hope. Perhaps there was a way out of her dark past, a chance to start anew and find peace. She decided to trust Lily and confided in her about the final job she had accepted.

Lily nodded, understanding the gravity of Brenda's situation. "The perfect crime doesn't exist, Brenda, but the perfect getaway might. It's not about escaping the consequences of your actions, but about choosing a different path and making amends for your past. There's goodness in you, and I believe you can still find redemption."

With Lily's guidance, Brenda devised a plan. Instead of carrying out the hit, she would use her skills to expose the true villains and bring them to justice. The contract was a trap set by a powerful criminal organisation seeking to eliminate any potential threats. Brenda would turn the tables on them and use the information she had gathered to dismantle their empire.

As Christmas Eve approached, Brenda set her plan in motion. With Lily's support, she unveiled the truth about the organisation's nefarious activities, implicating its leaders and ensuring that they faced the consequences of their actions. It was a dangerous game, and Brenda knew she was risking everything, but the chance for redemption was worth it.

On Christmas morning, as the sun rose over Bakersfield, Brenda received a surprise gift – her freedom. The organisation had been taken down by the authorities, and she was no longer their target. The weight on her shoulders lifted, and for the first time in years, Brenda felt a glimmer of hope.

As the town celebrated Christmas with joy and laughter, Brenda walked through the snow-covered streets, her heart filled with gratitude. She found Lily once more and thanked her for guiding her toward the path of redemption.

"You have given me the greatest gift," Brenda said, tears welling up in her eyes. "A chance to be more than just a killer, a chance to find goodness in my heart."

Lily smiled warmly. "The choice was always yours, Brenda. I merely helped you see the possibilities within yourself."

With a newfound sense of purpose, Brenda decided to stay in Bakersfield, to embrace the spirit of Christmas and dedicate her life to helping others. She used her skills to protect the innocent, to bring justice to those who needed it, and to honour the memory of those she had lost.

And so, Brenda Winters found her redemption, not through a perfect crime, but through a perfect getaway from her dark past. As the years passed, the legend of the assassin who became a protector spread through Bakersfield, and she became known as the woman who found salvation with the help of Santa Claus himself – a symbol of hope and goodness, guiding her toward a brighter future.

LOVE IS ALL YOU NEED
William Samson

Once upon a time, in a little town plagued by a mischievous troublemaker named Jack, things were about to take a bit of a turn. Jack, at the ripe old age of twelve, had the peculiar hobby of playing pranks on everyone he could find. His friends were fleeing from him faster than a cat from a cucumber. They couldn't handle his relentless antics anymore.

This tearaway had no boundaries. He stole chickens, adorned the church with graffiti like an abstract artist gone wild, and even managed to sneak whoopee cushions onto the mayor's chair during serious city council meetings. Oh, the chaos!

But there was one person who had enough of Jack's shenanigans, the no-nonsense lawman, Sheriff Billy. This stern sheriff, feared by wrongdoers, was tired of being a laughing stock due to Jack's endless pranks. Sheriff Billy knew he had to catch the young prankster red-handed and make him pay for his deeds.

Enlisting the help of a private investigator, Sheriff Billy was finally able to gather irrefutable evidence of Jack's latest caper. The evidence was damning. Jack had stolen the sheriff's beloved cow and painted it bright pink! Oh, the humiliation! The townsfolk couldn't contain their laughter, and Sheriff Billy's reputation hit an all-time low.

Fuelled by rage and a desire for revenge, Sheriff Billy plotted his plan to teach Jack a lesson. But in his pursuit of justice, Sheriff Billy started to lose sight of his high morals. Uh-oh, this was about to get serious.

One fateful day, Jack received an intriguing anonymous letter, an invitation to a "secret meeting" in the town's abandoned mine, at midnight! The excitement was palpable, and Jack couldn't resist a good adventure. Little did he know, the letter was not sent by a fellow prankster but by the vengeful Sheriff Billy himself.

When Jack arrived at the mine, a group of people awaited him in the shadows. Before he could utter a word, he was unexpectedly greeted with a rock to the head. Ouch! That wasn't part of the plan.

Jack woke up in a cold, dark cell, devoid of windows. It dawned on him that he had been kidnapped by none other than Sheriff Billy and his cronies. Sheriff Billy had officially gone off the deep end.

Days turned into nights, and Jack endured endless torture and interrogations, all while Santa's magical night drew near. And then, on the third night of his imprisonment, amidst the moon's eerie glow, a faint jingling sound reached Jack's ears. He blinked in disbelief as Santa Claus himself materialised in front of him, a cloud of magical dust and a hearty "Ho, ho, ho!"

"Santa? Is this for real?" Jack stammered, his jaw almost hitting the floor.

"Oh, indeed, my boy," Santa chuckled. "I couldn't let a young lad like you spend Christmas Eve locked up. So, here I am, spreading some holiday cheer!"

As Santa shared heartwarming stories of children from around the world, naughty and nice, Jack couldn't help but feel a connection. Santa's compassion and understanding touched him deeply.

"You know, Jack," Santa said gently, "sometimes kids act out because they crave love and attention. But being naughty won't get you what you truly desire."

Tears welled up in Jack's eyes. Santa was right; he had been seeking attention in all the wrong ways. The magic of Christmas was teaching him a valuable lesson.

Santa offered Jack a special gift, a Christmas wish. Jack pondered for a moment. He could ask for anything, but he knew exactly what he needed most, a parent's love and guidance.

"I wish for the love of a parent, someone to care for me and show me the way," Jack said, his voice resolute.

Santa nodded approvingly. "A wise choice, my dear boy. Love is the most precious gift of all."

With a burst of magical glow, the cell lit up with warmth and affection. Jack felt an overwhelming sense of love surrounding him. In that moment, he knew his wish had come true.

Santa patted Jack's back and stood up. "Remember, Jack," Santa said with a twinkle in his eye, "carry the spirit of love and kindness in your heart, even after this magical night." And with that, Santa vanished, leaving Jack with newfound hope.

Sheriff Billy packed away his red suit and snook off back into town, let himself into his house and settled down with a well earned mince pie and a glass of milk. And Jack never did hear from Sheriff Billy again after that night.

From that day forward, Jack's life changed for the better. He found a loving family who embraced him with open arms, guiding him toward a life filled with love and joy.

As the years passed, Jack shared his magical night with others every Christmas, spreading the message of love, compassion, and the enchantment of Christmas to all who would listen. And through his tales, he kept the spirit of Santa alive in his heart, all year round.

So, dear friends, remember that love and kindness can turn even the naughtiest tearaway into a beacon of light. And should you ever need a little magic, just believe in the spirit of Christmas, for it might lead you to an unexpected adventure of love and transformation!

MEET THE AUTHORS

This, dear reader, is your chance to get to know a tiny snippet of information about some of our contributing authors:

Daizi Rae: 'A Nottingham lass, currently living in Derby, I've always had an adventurous spirit.

Together with the 'delightful' April Berry, (don't laugh!) I co-host the Bare Books podcast, weaving together literary wonders for our listeners.

In my moments of relaxation, you'll often find me immersed in the chilling worlds created by the likes of Stephen King, Clive Barker, and Dean Koontz. Books have been my lifelong passion, and I find solace in the pages of thrilling tales that transport me to other realms. Join me on my literary journey, the adventure never ends, and there's always room for one more thrilling story!'

Also by Daizi Rae:
Dukki: The Adventures of a Fireduck.
Featured in *Bare Books Anthology Volumes 1 and 2.*

Sandy Biddles: 'I am a retired primary teacher with a BA Hons in English/Psychology and other random certificates, a mum, a nanny and dog lover, also an avid reader of a range of genres – particularly historical fiction. I have been scribbling for a long time, these anthologies are the first works I have attempted to be published in.'

Also by Sandy Biddles:
Featured in *Bare Books Anthology Volume 2.*

Carolyn Ward-Daniels: Carolyn was born on the Derbyshire, Nottinghamshire border and has lived in both counties in equal measure. She completed four full-time years at college to leave with a degree in industrial art and design specialising in interiors. Her working life has been in this design field and any spare time after sleeping is spent writing and painting. Her weakness is cake, vodka, books and guitars in that order.

Also by Carolyn Ward-Daniels:

August.

Flint.

The Flint Babies.

Pelham.

Featured in *Bare Books Anthology Volumes 1 and 2.*

April Berry: April is a Yorkshire lass who moved south 25 years ago and has stayed put. She is mum to 2 fur babies, and can often be found cycling round Nottinghamshire in her spare time or listening to Motown or Soul music, sometime both at the same time. An avid reader since she could hold a book, Enid Blyton in childhood, moving on to the Constable books, John Grisham, James Patterson and Lee Child amongst her favourite authors. The day jobs have concentrated around food with a side way shift to employment issues latterly. April never considered writing until just recently, cajoled and chivvied into it by her co-presenter on Bare Books podcast, where, along with Daizi, she can be found reviewing all that is good from Independent authors.

Also by April Berry:

Featured in *Bare Books Anthology Volumes 1 and 2.*

Gerry O'Keeffe: 'Writer, podcaster and all round Sci-Fi and Crime Fiction geek.' Gerry also writes under the pen name of Benny O'Caffery. You can learn more about Gerry at: 7ardis.wordpress.com

Also by Gerry O'Keeffe:

Another Halloween Mess - writing as *Benny O'Caffery.*

Featured in *Bare Books Anthology Volumes 1 and 2.*

Jayne Love: Jayne was born in Harrogate, and bought up in Studley. She now lives in Manchester but remains always proud of her Yorkshire roots and accent - even if that accent is now peppered with Mancunian colloquialisms. Jayne is the epitome of a crazy cat lady! She was also one of our original writers for the Bare Books Podcast.
Also by Jayne Love:
Featured in *Bare Books Anthology Volumes I and 2.*

Finbar Ansbe: Finbar was born and raised in Brighton. He is one sixth of Cheap Dirty Horse, a rowdy, queer trash, folk-punk, dad kissing band from Nottingham. Finbar is mostly a song-writer but sometimes dabbles in poetry and short stories too.
Ali Smith, Jeff Mangum, and Raphael Bob-Waksberg are particular inspirations of his.

Ceejhay Walker: 'my love for fiction writing and reading especially paranormal romance, fantasy, mystery and suspense genres know no bounds. I channeled this love towards fiction GhostWriting and it's been going extremely well. However, out here in the real world I'm not just a fiction writer but a student architect as well. Doing two extremely different careers is not only challenging, but interesting.'

Dean Wrigley: 'A born and bred Bedfordian with a dash of Adelaide included in the mix. In 2020 I was thrilled when Daizi asked whether I would like to contribute a story to the podcast. My first story was about my cat. A reader of classics and now an amateur writer of flash. A lover of animals, chocolate and procrastination.'
Also by Dean Wrigley:
Featured in: *Bare Books Anthology Volumes I and 2.*

To everyone that downloads
and listens to the podcast.
To all the contributing authors
that made this book possible.
And especially to you
for buying and reading this book.

We couldn't do any of it without you.

THANK YOU